D0195061

blue
rider
press

RADIO FREE
VERMONT

RADIO FREE VERMONT

VERMONT

A Fable of Resistance

BILL McKIBBEN

BLUE RIDER PRESS

NEW YORK

blue
rider
press

An imprint of Penguin Random House LLC
375 Hudson Street
New York, New York 10014

Blue Rider Press is a registered trademark and its colophon is
a trademark of Penguin Random House LLC

Page 225 constitutes a continuation of this copyright page.

Library of Congress Cataloging-in-Publication Data
Names: McKibben, Bill, author.
Title: Radio Free Vermont : a fable of resistance / Bill McKibben.
Description: New York : Blue Rider Press, [2017]
Identifiers: LCCN 2017009744 (print) | LCCN 2017014871 (ebook) |
ISBN 9780735219878 (EPub) | ISBN 9780735219861 (hardcover)
Subjects: LCSH: Government, Resistance to—Fiction. |
Secession—Vermont—Fiction. | Counterculture—Fiction. |
Vermont—Fiction. | Political fiction. | BISAC: FICTION / Humorous. |
FICTION / Literary. | FICTION / Political. |
GSAFD: Humorous fiction. | Satire.
Classification: LCC PS3613.C5588 (ebook) |
LCC PS3613.C5588 R33 2017 (print) |
DDC 813/.6—dc23
LC record available at https://lccn.loc.gov/2017009744
p.   cm.

Printed in the United States of America
1   3   5   7   9   10   8   6   4   2

BOOK DESIGN BY AMANDA DEWEY

For Spunky Knowsalot

RADIO FREE
VERMONT

1

The morning crowd at the Bennington Starbucks moved through the time-honored rituals with rote familiarity: ordering their caffeine and caramel in pidgin Italian, waiting like schoolkids for their names to be called, and then either exiting into the faintly cool January air or sinking childlike into an oversized, overplushed armchair for a hit of the Web. The stereo played, over and over, the same nine songs by aging— aged, actually—guitar hero Peter Frampton, now appropriately acoustic.

Then, right in the middle of some melancholy chord, a voice crackled over the sound system, a voice that some people in the coffee shop immediately recognized. "Greetings, Green Mountain Starbuckers," said Vern Barclay in his deep radio baritone with just a hint of his Franklin County upbringing. "This is a special message going out just to those of you in the nineteen Vermont shops. The other 34,513 Starbucks scattered across the planet Earth and aboard our lazily orbiting space station will continue to listen to Mr. Frampton mark the launch of his new album on Starbucks' label. I know that all of us join in thanking the coffee giant for taking the musical icons of our various youths and encouraging them to noodle acoustically in the background, and it is a great pleasure to know that no matter which shop you visit, the soundtrack will be the same—it's almost as reassuring as the muffled *bu-dump bu-dump* of the womb. But today, your friends here at Radio Free Vermont, 'underground, underpowered, and underfoot,' wanted to take this opportunity to patch into the streaming Starbucks signal and remind you that we still have coffee shops in this state actually owned by Vermonters. Coffee shops where the money in the till doesn't disappear back to Seattle, where the cream in the Mocha-Sexy CappaMolto comes from the cow down the road, and where the music on the stereo might actually come from your neighbors. You can find a list at RadioFreeVermont.org, if the authorities haven't managed to shut it down today, and don't bother telling them Vern sent you—they'll know. Remember: small is kind of nice. And now—if perhaps your barista will be so kind as to turn up the volume a notch or two—we leave you with a little Grace Potter and the Nocturnals, straight out of Waitsfield."

As it happened, the manager was actually up on a stool trying to turn the speakers off. But not before Grace Potter's

voice on the chorus of "Ah, Mary" cut through the morning air:

Ah, Mary
She'll bake you cookies then she'll burn your town
Ah, Mary
Ashes, ashes but she won't fall down

Meanwhile, about sixty miles north, a beer truck lum-
bered slowly off the Crown Point Bridge and began the drive
up Route 22 toward Burlington. It hadn't gone a mile before
the driver came to an orange detour sign in the middle of the
road, and turned left on a dirt farm road. He drove about a
mile more, past cows staring impassively at the sides of his
truck with its pictures of two young women in bikinis, reclin-
ing in a hot tub and hoovering Coors Light long necks with
an ardor that suggested deep and full-bodied pleasure. Around
a bend in the road, the truck driver found another detour
sign, and followed it for two miles, till yet another sign guided
him down a dirt road next to a creek lined with willows, a
creek still flowing in the mild January chill. After about a mile
of that—with the road turning into rut—he came upon a lady
in a balaclava holding a Stop sign. The driver braked, and as
he did two young men—also in balaclavas—appeared, one on
either side of the truck. Each had a tire pressure gauge, and
within seconds air was hissing out of the front tires and the
truck slumped slightly forward.

"Apologies," said the lady in the balaclava. "This will take a little while, I'm afraid. If you wanted to walk to the nearest house and call the police that's fine, but it's about four miles. Or you could wait a little while, and then we'll fill your tires again. Anyway we've made you a picnic." She put a paper sack on the seat beside him and started lifting things out. "BLT, with bacon from Vermont Smoke and Cure. A whole pint of Strafford Creamery maple walnut ice cream. And here's something special: a bottle of the new Long Trail Coffee Stout in Bridgewater Corners. The coffee doesn't come from Vermont, but it is roasted here—you can only have one, because we're serious about DUI in this state, but I think you'll find it filling. And we've got a gift pack of beers from fifty-one of Vermont's brewers to send home with you! Did you know we had more breweries per capita than any place on earth? I have no idea why they think we need Coors too." While she talked—the driver just gaped—the two young men were busy hauling down cartons of beer. They opened each, quickly twisted the caps, and then turned the whole box upside down to drain. When the bottles were empty, they loaded the cartons into the back of two pickups.

The driver watched from his rearview mirror, and after about half an hour he finally spoke:

"Hey, lady. This is going to take forever—I've got twelve hundred cartons in the truck. Why don't you just toss them over the side and let me go?"

The woman looked up at him from above a draining carton of beer. "Oh, sweetie," she said. "This is Vermont. We *recycle*."

Three hours later they were done. The balaclava-clad men pumped up his tires with a 12-volt air compressor and then disappeared into the small clayplain forest at the edge of the farm driveway; the woman thanked the driver and then disappeared herself. He couldn't think what else to do, so he started his truck and headed back toward the bridge and his home in New York, forty-eight hundred bottles of Coors Light-er but with an impressive stack of cases of Vermont microbrew. The Holsteins stared at him with the same unimpressed gaze, even though the ladies on the side of the truck now sported large talk balloons above their heads.

"My breasts are suspiciously large," one was saying to the other.

"As are mine, and this beer tastes quite watery," replied her tubmate.

<hr/>

The seventh grade of Harwood Union High School hunched over their laptops, waiting for the next problem set. In the morning, like every other seventh grade in the state and indeed the nation, they'd finished three modules of science questions in the monthly EYE (Every Youth Enhanced) tests mandated by the federal Department of Education. Now they were waiting for the beep that would signal the start of the American history section. A Distance Learning Specialist, highly trained both to reboot connections and block students from accessing anything interesting on the Internet, watched from his desk in the front of the room.

The digital tone rang, and the screens all set to the first question:

THE U.S. GOVERNMENT IS COMPOSED OF THREE BRANCHES.

A. The legislative, the executive, and the President
B. The executive, the judicial, and the Supreme Court
C. The legislative, the Congress, and the Bill of Rights
D. The legislative, the judicial, and the executive

Before even the swiftest could toggle the answer, though, the screens went blank and then were instantly replaced with a new set of questions, blinking in the same font:

GREETINGS, YOUNG VERMONTERS. THIS DAY, THE 21ST OF
JANUARY, 2018, IS THE BIRTHDAY OF

A. Ethan Allen, hero of Ticonderoga and captain of the Green
   Mountain Boys
B. Gov. Leslie Bruce, hero of nothing
C. Ben
D. Jerry

WHEN ETHAN ALLEN CAPTURED THE CANNON AT TICONDEROGA FROM THE BRITISH, HE SAID WHAT TO THE COMMANDER OF THE IMPERIAL FORCES:

A. That he came "in the name of the Great God Jehovah and the Continental Congress"
B. "Come out here, you damned old rat."
C. "Come out of there, you sons of British whores, or I'll smoke you out."
D. All of the above

ETHAN ALLEN, WHILE VERMONT WAS STILL AN INDEPENDENT RE-PUBLIC, WROTE A BOOK ATTACKING THE PURITAN ORTHODOXY OF THE DAY. IN IT HE SAID THAT THOSE WHO BELIEVED THAT CHRIS-TIANS WERE "THE FAVORITES OF HEAVEN EXCLUSIVELY" WERE "NARROW AND BIGOTED." WHEN ETHAN ALLEN DIED, THEREFORE, PROMINENT AMERICANS SAID OF HIM:

A. "Ethan Allen of Vermont died and went to hell this day."
B. "He was an awful infidel, one of ye wickedest men ye ever walked this guilty globe. I stopped and looked at his grave with a pious horror."
C. "The mortal remains of Ethan Allen, fighter, writer, states-man, and philosopher, lie in this cemetery. His spirit is in Vermont now."
D. All of the above

SINCE TODAY IS ETHAN ALLEN'S BIRTHDAY (REMEMBER—READ CAREFULLY TO ANSWER ALL QUESTIONS), YOUR FRIENDS AT

RADIOFREEVERMONT.ORG ARE PLEASED TO INFORM YOU THAT THE REST OF TODAY'S TESTING HAS BEEN CANCELED. ON YOUR WAY OUT THE DOOR, PLEASE THANK THE DISTANCE LEARNING SPECIALIST FOR HIS OR HER HARD WORK ON BEHALF OF YOUR EDUCATION. SHOULD HE OR SHE PROTEST YOUR DEPARTURE, PLEASE QUOTE MR. ALLEN: "EVER SINCE I ARRIVED TO A STATE OF MANHOOD, I HAVE FELT A SINCERE PASSION FOR LIBERTY."

2

"Explain to me again why they can't trace our location?" Vern Barclay asked. A thin and graying man, he sat in a small, book-crammed study, slightly slouched over the microphone on the rolltop desk before him.

The question was addressed to a young man, on his knees beneath the desk, who was disconnecting a pair of alligator clips from a telephone jack.

"Well, because wireless?" said Perry Alterson, rapidly coiling the short length of cable and stowing it in a yellow toolbox. As Alterson rose, his dreadlocks drooped down toward his shoulders. He was lanky—skinny, really—and pale; Aretha Franklin's profile peered from his T-shirt.

"When the Internet began," Perry continued, "people had dial-up? Which for a year or two seemed very fast and then it seemed very slow? So we got cable, DSL, satellite—'broadband.' By now, even in Vermont there's nothing but high-speed?"

"Remind me again when you got out of high school," said Vern. "Actually, don't remind me."

"I didn't completely get out?" said Perry. "I mean, I stopped going a couple of years ago, but I'm not—I didn't have that much in common with my classmates?"

"That seems possible," said Vern. "Anyway—the Internet."

"So, the whole system is insanely fast now. That's why you can download a two-hour movie in four seconds? But all the old architecture is still underneath. They didn't replace it, they just built over it. As long as you've got the old hardware, you can still go right through a phone jack and into the 'net. It's . . . retro? And that's what garage sales are for." He held up an ancient rectangular modem, green light blinking slowly, then reached down to disconnect it from the wall and coiled the wire before adding it to the toolbox.

"The thing is," Perry continued, "the authorities spend all their time trying to out-hack the latest hackers? They've got gear that can follow every pulse of light down a fiber-optic cable in a nanosecond? That's why our website is down more often than it's up. It takes every trick I can think of to keep Radio Free Vermont from disappearing altogether. It's why you have to do podcasts, nothing live: they'd be through our door in half an hour? But when it's like this morning, and all we need to do is appear for a few minutes out of nowhere and then vanish, then the old copper wires are just fine. And none of their tracing equipment even notices—it's tuned for fast, not slow?"

"It's like they've blockaded the airport and we're at the train station," said Vern, as much to himself as to Perry. "Did you know that a hundred years ago you could get to almost every town in Vermont on the train? You ever notice how even little hamlets come with a depot down by the common? Most of them are art galleries now, but a depot implies a train, does it not? A train pulling in every few hours and heading up the valleys, across the mountains, down to New York, up to Montreal. A civilized thing, a train."

"Anyway," said Perry. "Don't ask me to send video across the copper? Pause, pause, buffer, buffer—that's why they switched, really. If you want to have TV on a computer, the phone lines won't do."

"No need for pictures," said Vern. "We're quite old school."

"Which reminds me," said Perry, a little hesitantly. "The Grace Potter song? It rocked? But do you think maybe, since we're doing a radio station, we could play something that . . . I don't know."

"What are you thinking of?" Vern asked.

"Well," said Perry, looking down at his shirt. "Aretha. Or Etta James. Or Isaac Hayes. Or LaVern Baker. Or Fontella Bass. Or Nina Simone. Or Curtis Mayfield—did you know *Superfly* was number seventy-two on the *Rolling Stone* list of the five hundred greatest albums? Or—"

"I don't think any of them are from Vermont," said Vern.

"Almost no soul singers are from Vermont," said Perry. "Except Kat Wright and the Indomitable Soul Band. But how are we going to have a liberation struggle if all our supporters are listening to classical music on the public radio? I mean, we're supposed to be running a revolution here, not a pledge drive?"

"But we're supposed to be about Vermont," Vern said. "Vermont milk, Vermont beer, Vermont music."

"Milk and beer are *products*—they're supposed to be *fresh*? Music is an idea—it travels? And some of it lasts because it's . . . good." Perry, usually deferential, was becoming animated in a fashion Vern had never seen in their short time together. "I mean, are we only going to read books that get written in Vermont? Are we only going to look at paintings of *fall colors*? Curtis Mayfield wrote a song, 'Choice of Colors,' number five on the R&B chart. We *need* a choice of colors."

"Okay, next time," said Vern, but Perry had already taken the headphones from around his neck, placed them squarely over his ears, and walked out of the room, toolbox in hand.

Vern stared out the window, at a muddy paddock and beyond it the kind of second-growth hardwood forest he loved best. Normally, off the mike, he would have been out the door and into the woods—he'd spent the better part of his life, in all senses of the phrase, wandering the backcountry of Vermont.

But not today. For one thing, he was a wanted man. This was a secluded farmhouse at the end of a long dirt road and there wasn't much chance he'd run into anyone else, especially since Syl was away with the beer-truck caper and her classes were therefore canceled for the day. Still, his picture (and not a very flattering one, in his opinion) was up on every computer screen in the state, and there was no sense taking chances.

More than that, though, the sheer brownness of it all just depressed him. This was the middle of January, for most of his seventy-two years the happiest part of a happy year. When November came and the days grew short, his mood always began to soar. Cold meant snow and ice, and snow and ice meant: sliding. Meant the annual exemption from friction, meant that a solid Vermont farmboy became fast and agile. Graceful, almost, though when he'd been growing up that's not how he'd thought of it. "Lethal" was more like it: he'd grown up on cross-country skis, and he'd grown up deer hunting, and when he was a teenager, a neighbor had taught him to combine the two. Even then, biathlon—skiing and shooting—was never much of a big deal; he'd been far better known in high school for doing play-by-play of the basketball games on the local radio. But he was good on the snow, good enough to hang on to the bottom of the national team for a couple of years. Not Olympic years, which always made him a little sad, but medals had never been the point for him. It was the sheer painful pleasure of charging fast uphill on a pair of skis, legs pistoning, lungs sucking in air, skis slamming against a hard track. He'd coached the juniors from all around the state for years afterward. He was a better coach than an athlete, having sent several of his charges off to the Olympics. Trance, of course, the best of all—Trance, the once-in-a-lifetime athlete every coach waits for. "Giving back," he called it. But he'd done it mostly as an excuse to keep pulling on the boots and grabbing the poles and going off to . . . glide. It never stopped seeming unlikely and magical to him, the way friction just quit, and gravity turned from adversary to ally.

But no glide now, and not much for the last few years. The globe had warmed faster and harder than anyone had predicted. With Arctic ice melted, there was no place to build up the intense cold that had always marked winter in Vermont. Lake Champlain didn't freeze much anymore, and if snow fell, it was usually for a few nighttime hours in the middle of a rainstorm. He knew he should have been worrying about the people in Bangladesh busy building dikes to keep the sea at bay—but these warm muddy winters were what really bothered him about the change. No glide, just the suck of mud on his boots. It made him feel old, as if he'd outlived the very climate of his life, and it made him feel mad, and it made him feel tired. He lay back on the couch next to the desk, propped his hands behind his head, and settled in for a nap.

3

Maybe it was the afternoon nap; maybe the lack of exercise; but Vern Barclay slept poorly that night, and was wide awake by five. By long habit he flipped on the radio next to his bed, but the first thing he heard was a weather report (rain, in the low fifties) and the next was a nationally syndicated chat guy describing the quality of his orgasms from the previous night, and neither one cheered him up. He clicked it off and lay in bed, listening to nothing and then to the faint sound of tires on mud coming up the mile-long drive. He knew, as a wanted man, that he should probably go hide in the basement till Perry had figured out who it was, but in his current mood, capture didn't seem so awful, and he knew that Perry was pretty sure to be asleep with his headphones on. Anyway, he was growing more confident he recognized the slightly under-powered whine of a Subaru Outback, which would mean

Sylvia returning from her fun with the beer truck. Which meant, in turn, coffee and papers.

"Hi, friend," he greeted her as she climbed out of the car, still in her Carhartts, looking rumpled and a little gray. She'd clearly slept in the backseat after making sure her two helpers had gotten safely home, and she barely grunted as she walked past on her way toward the shower. But she had copies of the *Free Press* and the *Times Argus*, and she had a paper cup of Vermont Coffee Company coffee and a piece of crumb cake, all of which she handed off as she shuffled by.

Vern had been eating breakfast with these newspapers for more than half a century. Most of the time it was with a microphone open in front of him, and the news columns as a text to guide his show: obituaries first, local news, state news, milk prices, and if there was time, a mention of the national headlines. By his journalistic credo, something happening in, say, Oregon had to be pretty big before it mattered as much as an arson fire at a barn in Ferrisburgh. The Red Sox score was obligatory, of course, but followed quickly by Harwood Union boys' lacrosse and Otter Valley field hockey. So he eyed the newspapers professionally, as a baker might regard the bran muffins in a restaurant in a town where he was vacationing. It was, as always, a mild shock to see his own name in the headline ("A Voice from Nowhere: Barclay Fills Starbucks Airwaves"), and he did not like that damned file picture. But he read the story with interest—and when Perry wandered sleepily into the kitchen, he read it again, this time out loud.

"Listen to . . . this," he said, pausing for a second between "to" and "this." After decades on the air, he was locally famous for his pauses—for the intimacy they provoked, as the listeners would lean forward toward their radios a hair, caught a bit off-step. It was a trick he'd stolen from Paul Harvey, and in any event it didn't seem to work on Perry, who kept stirring his eggs, but still the habits of fifty years were hard to break. "Secession Capers Roil Local Schools, Merchants." A three-column picture showed students flooding out of Montpelier High even as the principal tried to shoo them back in, a look of alarm across his face. "Happy Ethan Allen Day, whoever he is," one tenth-grade scholar told the reporter, who also quoted several commuters who said they'd decided to break their Starbucks habit.

"Listen here, Perry, I think you'll enjoy this," Vern continued.

"*At an afternoon press conference, state police commissioner Tommy Augustus said the manhunt for Barclay would continue, and that authorities had added 'unlawful school dismissal' to the long list of charges the fugitive radio host already faced. 'This is an act of irresponsibility,' the commissioner said. 'Children could easily have been hurt when they were turned loose in the streets.'*

"*Asked if yesterday's string of escapades challenged their theory that Barclay was acting alone, Augustus said, 'He is an experienced communications professional. We think he is fully capable of manipulating the Web in this fashion, but the public should rest assured that the FBI is assisting us in the search and that with their technical capabilities we believe he will be captured shortly.'"*

Perry turned from the range and opened his mouth to speak, but then stopped. "I know what you're thinking," said Vern. "I may be an experienced communications professional, but I am not even fully capable of manipulating a coffee-maker. I'm the guy who couldn't figure out how to turn on the automatic reply so he could let people know he had gone into hiding and wouldn't be answering their e-mails."

"It's okay," said Perry. "I just thought newspapers got things right?"

"I'm sorry you're not getting full credit. I'd send Tommy Augustus a note, but I'm not sure he can even *open* e-mail. He's the state police commissioner because he drove the governor's car for two terms and was extremely good at not noticing which lobbyists were slipping in and out of the backseat. 'Not noticing' may not be the first thing you'd look for in a police chief, but in the Bruce administration it's an essential skill."

"But what about the beer? Have they noticed that yet?" asked a voice from the next room. Before he could answer, Sylvia Granger strode into the kitchen, and this time Vern's pause was involuntary. No more Carhartts, no more ponytail. Syl, all five-feet-two of her, wore a set of cherry-red snow-mobile leathers, as form-revealing as winter clothing gets. A cascade of blond hair, wet from the shower, fell halfway down her back.

"What's the matter? You look like you've never seen a

teacher before," she said. "Okay, the snowmobile suit is a little hot for this weather. But it's the first day of semester, and it's got the school logo on it, and anyway I hardly got to wear it a dozen times before the snow started disappearing. Which reminds me—class starts at noon, so get out of sight by eleven-thirty. And what about the beer?"

She pulled a glass jar of granola off the counter as Vern began to read:

"*Brattleboro brewer Angus McTavish told police he had no idea how his beer had ended up inside the Coors truck, Windham County troopers said yesterday. Reached at his brewpub last evening, however, McTavish said he considered it a 'major public service,' adding that beer was 'a living thing.'*

"'*What would you feel like if you'd been stuck in a truck and driven across the continent?' asked McTavish. "That's what beer from Colorado feels like," he said, adding that he now plans to brew a special batch of LiBeerTy Ale to help promote the secessionist cause.*"

"Good for Angus," said Sylvia.

"Beer really is like liquid bread," said Vern. "You wouldn't send bread in a truck from Mexico. Or probably you would, if you were a big company and could find a bunch of cheap bakers. But you shouldn't."

"Remember," said Syl. "Eleven-thirty."

4

Indeed, by eleven-thirty, the first few cars—hybrids, mainly—had begun to arrive, and Vern and Perry had secured themselves upstairs in the studio.

"I downloaded questions last night—the site was up for a few minutes on a mirror somewhere in Turkey," said Perry.

Vern had no idea what Perry was talking about, but he said, "Let's remember to be nice to Turkey once we've joined the UN. Maybe they need cheese. What do we have in the mailbag?"

"Well—one guy compared you to Benedict Arnold and Barry Bonds? A history guy and a baseball guy? Lots of 'What happens to my Social Security if we leave the U.S.?' The best one came from someplace called Derby Line."

"You've never been to Derby Line?" asked Vern. "Right up on the Canadian border? The line right down Main Street?"

"I didn't travel much?" said Perry. "Anyway, you'll like this one. 'Dear Vern: I've been listening to you every morning for my whole life. We'd keep the radio on in the barn during milking. All the cows loved it—they'd get nervous when you went on vacation. I'm not really a politics person, and I haven't followed all the back-and-forth, but I seriously doubt that you are a terrorist. I want to hear the story from your own mouth, the way you used to tell stories every morning.'"

Vern paused for a moment, pressed his hands together as if in prayer, brought his index fingers to his nose. "Press the button," he told Perry, glancing at the whiteboard propped against the wall.

"Hello, friends, and welcome to broadcast number six from Radio Free Vermont, underground, underpowered, and underfoot. We're brought to you today by Lawson's Brewery in the Mad River Valley, where there's always a 'Sip of Sunshine' to be had. When I say 'brought to you by,' I'm not implying that they're paying us money or giving us free samples. I'm just saying that they, and the at least fifty-seven other Vermont breweries, are symbols of everything that's right and good about a free local economy, where neighbors make things for neighbors—and so they actually bother to give them some taste, body, and character. Remember, drink responsibly: if your ale doesn't hale from your county, then just say no.

"I don't know when you'll be listening to this podcast, but we're making it here in our undisclosed and double-secret location on a fine Vermont morning—fine for May, not so fine for January, since the ground is brown and the temperature is in the fifties. Still, we'd like to thank all those Remote Education Specialists, or whatever they're called, who gave our children some extra recess yesterday: a sound body goes with a sound mind, as Ethan Allen himself knew, since he once was able to throttle a full-grown catamount that leaped onto his back. If old Ethan hadn't taken sufficient recess, we'd still be part of New York. And I see from today's paper that the girls from Harwood Union beat U-32 on the ice last night— congratulations to the Highlanders on getting through the first half of the season unbeaten.

"In our broadcasts so far I've tried to explain a little bit about what an independent Vermont might look like, and I've maybe railed a little about tyranny and empire. I don't think they've been very good shows, to tell you the truth, and that's because, since we can't open up the phone lines, there's not much way for me to carry on a conversation, which is what radio should be about; I get carried away when it's just my own voice. But since I think that even Tommy Augustus might be able to track us down if I gave out our phone number, the best we can do is answer those e-mails that come in on the odd moments that our site goes up somewhere around the world. So keep sending them. Today's best comes from way up north in Derby Line, from a milkmaid of indeterminate age but undoubted beauty who asked me to drop the propaganda for a while and just tell the story of how I came to be here, sitting behind a microphone talking rebellion, and how my mug came to grace the wall of your local post office. It will take a while, so settle in—and remember that the good thing about these podcasts is you can just slide on ahead to the end if you're getting bored.

"I began talking into a microphone when I was sixteen, calling the basketball games at Bristol High. That was back before we started consolidating all the schools, about which don't get me started. I wasn't much good at first, partly because I'd usually go straight from the biathlon range to the gym; I liked both, but I was more interested in skiing than talking. And I was the worst homer you ever heard. But I got a little better, and after I got out of high school and put in my few years of trying to get to the Olympics, I went to work for WVRT, reading the news, playing records. Good records, I might add—these were the 1960s. I called a hockey game or a basketball game almost every night of the winter, and I couldn't wait till April because we carried the Red Sox and it meant I could spend summer evenings on my own—or, before long, with Fran, and then our kids. Life was as sweet as I could imagine, and it went on like that for many years.

"Vermont was changing, of course. All the small farms were going out, and new people were arriving—the back-to-the-land people. But I didn't pay too much attention, at least not until I started in on the morning talk show every morning. This was long before Rush Limbaugh or his type: I didn't shout, I didn't take positions, I just brought on interesting people to interview and I took phone calls. It was a conversation, and it went on for many years, and one of the things it taught me was that lots of Vermonters weren't as happy as I was. I heard, more and more as the years went on, from people who thought things were changing for the worse around here. Sometimes they'd blame it on the newcomers, and sometimes they'd blame it on politicians, but mostly what they seemed to me to be saying was that our communities were starting to fail. That the towns where we knew each other and looked out for each other weren't working so well anymore. Maybe people were too busy at their jobs, or too busy sitting in front of the television set—all I knew was that old people were lonely all of a sudden, and a lot of others were feeling on their own too. Vermont was becoming more like the rest of the country, is one way of saying it. There was money, and it was exciting, but it was also different.

"I suppose that those changes helped me in certain ways—there was never any shortage of people wanting to call in and talk, and sometimes I think it was because they didn't anymore have the friends, the people around town, to talk to instead. So I did my job, and watched Vermont change, and talked to everyone who was anyone, and knew where the bodies were buried, and my boys grew up and went off to school, and Fran and I grew middle-aged (middle-aged if I was planning to live to a hundred and thirty), and then she died and that was that. I'd spent my life in a comfortable bubble, a little bit of the old Vermont that was fading everywhere around me but which I'd never had to really leave behind.

"And so it would have ended if Bob Earle, the man who'd built WVRT, hadn't gone and died too, and his family had to sell the station for taxes. Now, he'd passed up a dozen chances to sell while he was alive, and we were about the only independent station left in the state, but there was just no way to keep it going even though we had high, high ratings. We got bought up by a conglomerate out of Oklahoma, of all places, that had two hundred and seventy-five stations, including four others in Vermont. They changed us to an all-talk format—no more records in the afternoon—and the rest of the talk came through a satellite dish they parked out back. They kept me on—maybe they figured I'd retire soon, and anyway they liked my market share. But the blocks of commercials kept getting longer, and there was no more local news team, and the thought of covering high school hockey would have made the new owners laugh if (A) anyone had ever met them and (B) they knew how to laugh, which I sincerely doubt. Cackle, maybe, as they counted their money.

"Anyway, I kept pretending I was still doing something useful. But it hurt to say goodbye to just about everyone else who worked at the station—even the ad salesmen got put out, because they had a selling team out there in Oklahoma that tracked down national accounts. They cut an hour out of my show every day to make room for *Mikey and Mickey in the Morning*, which was two young gentlemen from somewhere sunny that specialized in making ribald comments. I'm no prude—well, maybe I am, but I've never quite come to grips with the idea that you should get on the radio and discuss bosoms and flatulence. Anyway, it somehow made it hard to follow up with a discussion of, say, school boards. I should have just retired—I would have just retired—except that they got my goat. You may remember that our Senator Sanders—my favorite politician, your favorite politician, and the man who should have been president—was organizing what little opposition there was in Washington to a new rule that would have let the big media companies own even more radio and TV stations. I had him on to talk about it, and he said a few things about 'big media barons,' and my boss out in Oklahoma e-mailed me a memo saying the topic was off-limits from then on. Which was, believe it or not, the first time in my whole career that I'd ever been told not to talk about anything.

"Now, I suppose I could see their point. This was a law that would have cost them money, and they paid me. But I'd spent my whole career thinking of myself as my own man— not as an employee so much as something sort of like an artist or a writer. Not that I thought what I did was art exactly, though there's an art to it. But I found I didn't like being told what to talk about, and I found that it was enough to make me think in a political way for the first time in my life. That sounds odd to say, because I'd been talking about politics for fifty years, every day, and I had my opinions. But the way I saw the job, it was pretty important not to have those opinions too strongly. Like I say, I started before Rush Limbaugh—I would have been embarrassed to be a spokesman for some party, and I would have been embarrassed if everyone who called in felt like they had to parrot back my thoughts on everything. But I'd led a sheltered life, I suddenly realized—and the minute someone told me what not to say, I felt as if I had to say it. And I felt, too, as if I understood more than I ever had before about why people had been calling me for fifty years, and why they'd been feeling angrier and more helpless. I felt like I wasn't in Vermont anymore—my own idealized Vermont, where what mattered were your neighbors and your values. And I realized that a lot of you had been forced out of that nice place long before me.

"As I say, I should have retired and gone home and sat in my chair and read my books and ventured out on Friday nights for Middlebury hockey. But I felt the way some people feel when they have a sudden flash of religion. I wanted to spread the word. For a few weeks my guest list was heavy with local foods activists and sprawl opponents and so on. I'd interviewed them before, of course, but before I was always careful to see both sides of the question—I was a pretty good devil's advocate. And now I wasn't—I was a convert. But it didn't feel like talking was going to move the needle. If I wanted a different Vermont, I'd have to do something more than talk. And I felt like I wanted to run some risk. My wife was gone, and my kids were grown, and after fifty years of talking it suddenly seemed silly to just keep on chattering. I wanted to *do* something.

"Which was the same moment when the station manager

assigned me to broadcast from the opening of the new Walmart in Saint Albans. Now, I've done a million of these over the years: three hours at the new Hyundai dealership or the new appliance store or whatever. You interview the owner in little chunks in between records; it's kind of boring because how much can you really say about the selection of washers and dryers, but I was used to it, and I always saw old friends, and it was part of the job. But this Walmart was different. They'd been fighting over it for a decade—over the cornfield that got paved over, over the runoff from that pavement, over the traffic. And over what it was going to do to the downtown in Saint Albans. Some folks wanted it, because some folks are poor enough or bored enough that the thought of a cheap place to go and shop is nice. Some folks hated it. Didn't really matter. What mattered was that Walmart had lawyers enough and money enough and time enough to make sure that in the end it finally went in.

"Once I knew I was going to make the broadcast, I called a few friends of mine who'd been active in the opposition, and we hatched a little plan. And it was a good little plan—a joke, mostly, but with a barb. It worked well, too. I was roaming the store with my little portable broadcast unit, and I was interviewing the people who'd be running the different sections. The hardware guy described the cheap snow shovels, and the sporting goods guy described the cheap fishing rods. About what you'd expect. And then the nice lady in the women's clothing section described, at some length, *why* the clothes there were so cheap—she described the factories where the blouses were sewn and the wages of the people who did the sewing. If you missed it, the broadcast is archived on the Radio Free Vermont website—I was pretty good and deadpan if I say so myself. And the same with the fellow who happened to be managing the electronics department, and who explained just how much more electricity you could use simply by buying one of the enormous cheapo TV sets. There were five of what I'd guess you'd have to call 'plants' scattered around the store, and I'd gotten to three of them when I saw the store manager hustling my way across the vast floor. Someone had clearly called the station, and they'd called him, and I was about ready to sign off and plead ignorance when something happened that we hadn't planned. Or rather, I hadn't planned it. Someone had, who's standing here next to me, and I've almost forgiven him.

"The first I knew of it was the smell, which took me quickly back to the barnyards of my youth. The store manager smelled it too, and he stopped before he even reached me and started looking around. We both saw it at pretty much the same time—a kind of tide, maybe six inches high, of water moving across the store at a stately but determined pace. Brown water. It turns out, I have since learned, that if you know how to program the switches, you can make a sewer system reverse itself. Walmart had installed a particularly big pipe, because they had to somehow cope with the runoff that would come when a late-August thunderstorm dropped two inches of rain on all that endless parking. But right now that pipe had gone from an intake to an outflow, and from all across Saint Albans, the contents of five thousand commodes were emptying onto the wide concrete floor of this well-scrubbed new outlet of global commerce.

"My compatriot had, he later said, intended it as a kind of visual pun—a play on the fact that he considered the store to be a crappy venture marketing crappy merchandise, though 'crappy,' I must say, was not the word he used. I don't know why I'm not using his word, since the FCC probably doesn't care, except that I refuse to be Mikey or Mickey at this late stage in my career. Anyway, it was quite a sight and quite a smell, and by the time it reached us I knew that we were, metaphorically as well as literally, in deep excrement. I did a quick assessment of how much merchandise was stored at two feet or below in this store, a rough calculation, but enough to be sure that it passed by several orders of magnitude the seven hundred and fifty dollars that Vermont sets as the boundary between a misdemeanor and a felony. And so, at the age of seventy-two with a total of four speeding tickets to my name, I panicked. I grabbed my compatriot, and two pairs of hip waders from sporting goods, and we headed quickly to the exit, as the fire department arrived on the scene. We abandoned the waders as we climbed into my car, and we abandoned the car a little later since it had 'WVRT Mobile Studio' all over the side, and we made our way—elsewhere in Vermont. To some-place safe.

"And just as well, as it turned out. Since Governor Bruce, who was looking for a way to scare people enough to get re-elected yet again next fall, declared that this was 'an act of terrorism aimed at disrupting the Vermont economy' and called in the FBI, the EPA, and the Border Patrol. The last two were a bit of a stretch—he wanted the store named a hazardous waste site, but the EPA, which barely has any bud-get left anyway, told him it could be cleaned. The Border Pa-trol said that while the store was indeed near the border, the clear ringleader, which would be me, had spent his whole life in Vermont and hence was not their problem. But the FBI, I believe, are still on the job. And my picture, as the terrorist in chief, went out across the Web.

"After which—in for a dime, in for a dollar—we launched the movement for an independent Vermont. Not much of a movement, not yet—mostly just a website that's hard to find, a few small bands of allies scattered around the state, and an occasional action to galvanize the public, as for instance yes-terday's small escapades with the beer and the Ethan Allen exam and the wonderful Grace Potter. I'm not much of a rev-olutionary, and this was all an accident, but I can't say I'm sorry it happened. And I hope you will give my best to your cows in Derby Line."

Vern sat back in his chair, and Perry tapped the button on the keyboard that stopped the digital recording. "That was weird?" he said. "You just sat there and talked for half an hour, without a script, without anything."

"That's what I've been doing every morning for half a century," said Vern. "It's actually kind of easy once you're able to imagine someone in particular sitting and listening. I used to think about my wife; now I think about my mother, though I'm not certain she's good enough with the Internet to actually track us down."

"You know I'm still kind of sorry about the sewage," said Perry. "I hadn't really thought it through."

"If you'd have thought it through, I'd be sitting home reading my books, instead of holed up in a safe house wondering when Tommy Augustus will come walking through the door. So—thank you," said Vern.

5

The clock had just pushed past noon, and from downstairs they could hear class beginning—quite easily, in fact, since the walls were thin and Sylvia's voice was not. "Gentlemen—welcome to the School for New Vermonters," she said. "I am well aware that most of you are here because your buddies at the investment bank thought it would make a funny retirement present, or your wife saw a clip on CNN and thought it would be cute. That said, I take it very seriously.

"We here in Vermont are of two minds about newcomers—actually, a good many of us are of one mind, but that would make you sad to hear. Everyone agrees, however, that if you're determined to move here it would be better if you knew how to fit in, not cause trouble, and be a decent neighbor. Where you came from, neighbors didn't matter—everyone in your cul-de-sac could die of some plague overnight and your life would go on largely unaffected. But here, neighbors are more than decorative; Burlington, our only real city, has fifty thousand people—it's more like a neighborhood. And if you live in the country—and statistically Vermont vies with Maine as the most rural state in the Union—then neighbors get you out of scrapes. My job is to keep you from getting into scrapes, and to teach you how to help others who do. Jesus said 'Love your neighbors,' yes? Well, think of me as Jesus with a tow chain and a Stihl saw.

"Today we'll cover driving in the mud; before the month is out, we'll have cut down small trees, learned to drive the kind of pumper you'll find in most volunteer fire departments, chopped, split, and stacked cordwood for several of the older ladies in this town—what are you saying?"

Vern and Perry could hear someone faintly asking a question, and then Sylvia's answer, in the same booming tone.

"As a matter of fact, I wasn't born here. I was born on the Upper West Side, Seventy-second and West End Avenue, a block from Riverside Park and a block the other way from the Famous Dairy Restaurant, which my grandfather ran. But my parents moved here when I was four, part of the hippie migration. I wasn't much of a hippie, but I was a pretty good Vermonter—I joined 4-H and raised sheep. There's still plenty of New York in me, though, which is why I work so well with migrants. You could say I'm an interpreter.

"And since you're asking personal questions, let me answer another one you haven't asked. As usual, most of you are men—that's because women, I think, generally know how to fit into a community more easily. They're good at making friends. Anyway, despite the fact that I look remarkably good in my red snowmobile leathers, I don't want to go on a date with any of you, or get fixed up with your sons, for a number of reasons but chiefly because I am a lesbian. Those of you from Boston or New York will not find this very remarkable, but some of the rest may have journeyed here from places where people still think it's okay to, for instance, tell you not to get married if you want to marry another girl. You're entitled to your opinion, but Vermont was the first place in the Union to legalize civil unions. We live and let live, and if your opinion is different from that, you'd do best to keep it to yourself.

"Now, if everyone has signed their releases, let's head out to the field for mud-driving, which is a key skill now that mud season seems to last all winter. I want you to remember a few things. You don't need four-wheel drive; you need brains. Traction is your best friend, and when traction disappears, momentum is going to have to take its place. Once you're in those ruts, know which way your wheels are pointed, because you don't want to come out the other side and drive into the trees. And if it looks really bad, deflate your tires a bit. Those of you who don't know how to drive a stick should be ashamed of yourself, but if you stay after class we'll work on it."

Vern listened with a chuckle; he'd known Sylvia since the week she opened her school and he'd had her on his show. Perry listened with a kind of rapt awe. They watched through the window as a dozen cars, one after another, bogged down in the mud pit Sylvia had built by the back of the barn. Each time she climbed in the passenger seat and talked the driver through the hole—by the time they got out the other side they were smiling and shaking her hand.

"She yells at them but they still seem to like her?" said Perry.

"If you show people how to pull themselves out of a hole, they're apt to like you," said Vern.

6

The three of them were sitting on the patio behind Sylvia's house late the next afternoon. It was sixty degrees in the fading sun, and if it didn't qualify as freak weather—more like the new normal—it still unnerved Vern and Sylvia. Perry not so much—he was young enough that he'd grown up with odd winters and was inclined to think of a warm January day as something to enjoy, not an omen.

"I'm always glad when we get past chainsaw day," Sylvia was saying. "I mean, they look so cute in their brand-new Kevlar chaps and sleeve gauntlets and hearing protectors and safety goggles and hard hats and steel-toed boots, but once they start up the saws, no one can hear a word I say. I have to space them fifty yards apart so the most they can kill is themselves."

"They did seem a little . . . eager," said Vern.

"Today was the worst in a while—two doctors in this

group. Doctors take advice from no one. They figure that if someone pays them four hundred thousand dollars to read X-rays, they must know how to fell a tree. I mean, after all, a logger only makes twenty dollars an hour, right? How hard can it be? But if you read an X-ray wrong, it still takes the patient a couple of years to die, and someone else might even catch it along the way. If you don't bother to check what's in the path of the ash you're felling—as Dr. Keith Ervin, lately of Raleigh, North Carolina, almost demonstrated today—there's a pretty good chance it is going to twirl around and fall on you. No one else is going to catch it, and your demise will take about two seconds, though it would probably be painless. I'm not certain anyone would have missed him, but I'm virtually certain someone would have sued."

She reached over and refilled Vern's half-empty glass from a big bottle of Rock Art Extreme Vermont Pale Ale ("Guaranteed smooth, mellow, and so bitter every hole will pucker"). Perry had hardly touched his.

"Too strong for you?" asked Sylvia. "I should have saved some of that Coors Light."

"I'm not a big beer-drinker," said Perry. "I mean, I'm only nineteen."

"When I was nineteen . . ." said Vern, but he said no more, because it wasn't really true. When he was nineteen, he'd been a good boy, and also an athlete, and he'd mainly drunk milk from the family dairy. Still, Sylvia inspired a bit of showing off.

"If you weren't drinking beer in high school, what were you doing?" said Sylvia. "Don't mind my asking," she added, when Perry looked away. "I'd never met you before you showed up at my house smelling like sewage, and I'm curious. I know you don't get on with your parents or else you'd have to have figured out some way to call them. But who were your friends? What was your scene?"

"Not so many friends," said Perry. "I'm interested in computers? Not, like computer games, so much. Computers? Like, coding. And I'm extremely interested in soul music, especially the great Atlantic recordings from the 1960s and the Stax/Volt stuff, right up until, like, the mid-seventies. Not Motown—Motown is, like, too obvious? Don Covay. Archie Bell. The Mar-Keys, Joe Tex, Donny Hathaway, Rufus Thomas, Mavis Staples, Major Lance, Isaac Hayes, the Emotions. Like, the Memphis Sound. I mean, not just Stax, but like Hi Records, whose studio was down the street. Where Ann Peebles recorded 'Part Time Love' in 1969. And also Al Green, before he became the Reverend Al Green. And then—"

Sylvia held up a hand. "Two questions," she said. "Why soul music—why not whatever it was that everyone else was listening to?"

Perry paused. "Well," he said. "I think, because it was complete? Like, over? Not completely—I mean neo-soul, and like Raphael Saadiq. And D'Angelo? And Erykah Badu? But *classic* soul. When I was a kid I was interested in presidents, and in astronauts. Because they were, like, lists? I mean, I knew a lot about the astronauts and their missions and whatever, but all of it was *wrapped up*. It didn't have so much to do with now. You could know all of it."

"Second question—and remember, I'm blunt," said Sylvia, though she said it with considerable tenderness, facing him head-on. "Did you ever get tested?"

Perry looked at her. "Um, Asperger's?" he said. "Mild? Like, the doctor said no need for medication. He told my mother that I was 'socially inept,' and she said, 'That sounds like him.'"

"I know about Asperger's," said Vern. "I did several shows about it. It's most common in boys—"

"I don't think we need you going all Asperger's about Asperger's," she told Vern. "I bet Perry knows a good deal about it. I know a little. My brother more or less lived for the periodic table."

"I like the periodic table," said Perry, a little hesitantly. "But the doctor also said I'd outgrow some of it, and I think that's true. Like, with the music. When I first started being interested, it was, like, the dates and who left what group and joined which other group, and who produced what, and which house band backed what song, and—like, I'm still interested in all those things. But the more I listened, the more I paid attention to what they were talking about. Like sex, obviously, but also like peace and civil rights and stuff? It's how I ended up at that Walmart, actually."

"Do tell," said Sylvia. "I'd been wondering."

"Well, one day I was walking on Church Street Mall in Burlington, and I heard a stereo playing 'Say It Loud—I'm Black and I'm Proud,' which is one of my favorite songs—James Brown, 1968, peaked at number ten on the Billboard Hot 100, listed by *Rolling Stone* as number 350 of the five hundred most influential rock songs of all time, which I think is ridiculous. I mean, 'Walk This Way,' the Aerosmith–Run-DMC version was 287? You think?

"Anyway, I went into the store where the song was playing, and it turned out to be the Peace and Justice Center there on Church Street, and I got kind of involved in their stuff. I mean, opposing the war and all? I'd sit at the petition table? And then I kind of fixed up all their computer systems, which they pretty much needed. And one of them asked me to analyze the storm water runoff from the Walmart because they were protesting. She was a girl, actually? Which is how I learned about the sewer. And the rest . . ."

"The rest we know," said Sylvia. "And for what it's worth, I'm glad you're here. It's not exactly a proper home with proper parents, but . . . well, anyway," she said, shifting in her chair and turning her head quickly, "there's stuff we all need to talk about."

"Indeed," said Vern. "We need a council of—not war, exactly. It doesn't seem to me that we're exactly warriors."

"No, but we do need to figure out what we're going to do. I mean, going home doesn't seem like a great option for either

of you, and I am already home. And maybe we've got something going. Pretty much everyone in the convenience stores
has been talking about the kids getting out of school, and
most of them were laughing, like they thought it was kind of
cool. It seems to me we might actually be reaching people.
People are so freaked out by Trump they're looking for something to rally around."

"Yep," said Vern. "But what on earth do we do with it?
Every revolution I know about, they start by robbing some
banks. But we don't really need much money, do we? I can't
get at mine, but I'll pay you back for those cases of beer—that
was a good touch."

"Don't worry about it," said Sylvia. "This school actually
makes good money—there's really no limit what you can
charge people arriving from New York. Anyway, the other
thing real revolutionaries always do is take over the radio
station."

"Well, thanks to Perry, we more or less have," said Vern.
"Radio Free Vermont's not exactly a fifty-thousand-watt
powerhouse, but we're on the air and people can find the
signal. And judging by the e-mail, they are finding us."

"The thing is, when we put up a podcast it's not up very
long before they find the server we're using and shut it down,"
said Perry. "But there are friends of mine spreading whatever
we get up all over the place. I found yesterday's webcast on,
like, four thousand sites when I googled it this afternoon."

"Which means we better come up with something to say,"

said Vern. "None of us really started out to secede from the Union—when we called it Radio Free Vermont it was just because that's what you call such a thing. It was the newspapers that started in on secession. We were just—making a fuss. Sure, I suppose independence might be the logical extension of what we've been saying about bigness. But frankly I have no idea what it actually means. Five or six years ago there were some guys—I had them on the show—who were going on about leaving the United States. They liked to dress up as Ethan Allen and issue proclamations and such, but they fell in with a bunch of would-be Confederates down South, and pretty soon everyone forgot about the whole thing, and just as well. They were idiots, actually.

"See, that's the thing. If anyone's ever going to take this seriously, we need some way to make it seem real," he continued. "The beer stuff is actually good. We produce enough of it to satisfy our needs—we're beer-independent. But food, and energy, and jobs, and arts, and all that kind of stuff. I think we've gotten so used to the idea of the big enormous nation that we're a tiny part of, that it would scare most people to even imagine really breaking away. Like an eight-year-old running away. We need to convince folks that we're eighteen now, and it's time to strike out on our own. But it can't just be stunts. It's got to be facts, data, ideas."

"The best thing would be to have a debate," said Sylvia. "To get the governor on the other side."

"Something tells me the governor might decide not to,"

said Vern. "I mean, he only debates during election campaigns if he's worried about losing, and I don't think he's actually all that afraid of us right now."

"Well, we could stand in for him," said Sylvia. "You could do broadcasts and Perry could raise the arguments we think might bother people, and you could answer them."

"Better yet, I could raise the arguments and Perry could answer them," said Vern.

"I . . . don't like to talk?" said Perry.

"You are a facts-and-figures guy, though," said Vern. "I have a feeling that if you boned up for a little while you'd be able to cover almost anything. We could make you into a champion debater. And it would be a good idea too, because it's just possible people may have heard almost enough of me. I mean, I'm seventy-two years old and I talk on the radio every day. People expect me to be glib, and they expect me to be all choked up about the good old days and the small towns and the whatnot. You're nineteen—if you're making good arguments, it'll be considerably more impressive."

"I don't think anyone would pay much attention to me? No one ever has?" said Perry.

"Hon, there aren't many of us, and I can't go on the air because they don't know I'm part of this grand conspiracy just yet," said Sylvia. "That leaves the two of you. And I think you'll be great."

"If I was going to go on the radio, I'd rather play music," said Perry. "Could I play some after I talk?"

"I don't know," said Vern. "This should be serious—I mean, we're talking about the political future of Vermont."

"Actually, people like music a good deal more than politics," said Sylvia. "I think you should."

"But maybe not soul music?" said Vern. "Maybe something that's more about Vermont?"

"I think we should have a contest," said Perry, brightening. "An anthem contest. Every country has an anthem, we need one too. Every broadcast, we can play another possibility, and people can vote."

"Um, what were you thinking of?" asked Vern.

"Well, I wasn't. But maybe 'I've Got to Go On Without You,' William Bell, which never got higher than fifty-four on the R&B charts but it's a great record. Or 'Hey You! Get Off My Mountain,' by the Dramatics. That sounds like an independence song, right? I mean, it's perfect. 'Hey you—get off my mountain—you're just trying to bring me down.' And people liked it—Top Ten Rhythm and Blues charts, crossed over to the pop Top Fifty. 'Bring It Home,' by Hot Sauce, topped off at number thirty-five R&B. Mel and Tim, the guys who did 'Backfield in Motion,' had a great tune for Stax: 'Starting All Over Again.' I mean, 'Starting all over again is going to be rough, but we're gonna make it.' That's what you want, right? I mean, Sam and Dave wanted to release the song on Atlantic, what does that tell you, but the label said no. Top Twenty pop hit. The Staples Singers, all by themselves, did 'Be What You Are,' 'I Got to Be Myself,' and 'If

You're Ready Come Go with Me,' hit, hit, hit. Or what about 'Release Me,' Esther Phillips, which was actually a country-western song, Engelbert Humperdinck even recorded it, though I don't think any of us would want to live in a country with an Engelbert Humperdinck national anthem."

"Although when he released it, it kept 'Strawberry Fields Forever' out of the number one slot," said Vern—and when Perry looked at him with sudden, startled respect, he said, "Remember, I was a disc jockey. And actually, I think you're right—we need a contest. You can play your songs, but the listeners get to suggest their own too, right? I mean, this is going to be a democracy, isn't it?"

"We haven't talked about that," said Sylvia, opening a bottle of Otter Creek Couch Surfer Stout. "When you're drinking beer, go light to dark in the course of the evening," she said to Perry. "If it's a democracy maybe Governor Bruce will be elected president. Maybe we should have a monarchy."

"A queen for sure," said Vern. "If you can make radiologists pay you to cut down saplings with chainsaws, you can probably run a country."

"I imagine I could," said Sylvia. "But I imagine maybe we better have a democracy anyway. People are somewhat used to it."

"There's Ray Charles—'The Right Time,'" said Perry. "Like, this is the right time for independence."

"I don't think that's what that song was about," said

Sylvia. "'The night time is the right time,' if I recall," and Perry blushed.

"It's too bad we don't live in Georgia—'Georgia on My Mind' would be a good song," he said. "Number one, and the Grammy for best male vocal in 1960. But I guess it wouldn't make much sense for Vermont."

7

"Friends and neighbors," said Vern, "it's kind of you to tune in for the next in our Radio Free Vermont broadcasts. Today we're starting something different—and you'll be hearing a new voice. Perry 'Sewerman' Alterson will be delivering the first in a series of rigorous, straightforward, factual arguments for an independent Vermont—we don't want anyone just carried along for the ride on currents of emotion. Before we begin, our thanks to today's pseudo-sponsor, Kingdom Brewing, and their Lake Willoughby Lager, as refreshing as a midsummer dunk in that lovely lagoon. And if you're hearing this before Saturday, remember to stop by the United Methodist Church in Hyde Park for the annual white elephant sale, ten to four in the fellowship hall. If you e-mail us your community announcements here at Radio Free Vermont, we'll do our best to get them on the air.

"And now, Perry Alterson, on the question that's surely occurred to a few of you: Isn't little Vermont too little to simply strike out on its own?"

Vern swiveled smoothly in his chair and pointed at Perry, who lurched a few inches forward toward his microphone and began to talk—less talk, really, than blurt. He talked at the microphone instead of through it, like a man ordering from a drive-through, and there was a squeak at the top edge of his voice as he shuffled through the sheets on his desk.

"Vermont has 624,594 people," he began. "Twenty countries belonging to the United Nations have smaller populations. One small nation is San Marino. It is the oldest constitutional republic on earth. It was founded in 301 by a Christian stonemason fleeing persecution. It has 33,285 people. Their average annual per capita income is $65,300. That's twelfth in the world. Key industries are banking, electronics, wine, and cheese, also postage stamps.

"Another small nation is Luxembourg. It has 582,291 people. They average $102,000 annually, first in the world. They were a founding member of NATO, the European Union, and the United Nations. Because it is entirely surrounded by land, they have no navy."

Perry stalled for a second as he shuffled papers, but kept himself hunched in front of the mike. "Another small nation is The Bahamas. Which has 327,316 people. Their average income is $24,600, which is seventy-eighth in the world and third in the Western Hemisphere.

"Another small nation is Bhutan, population 750,125. It has—"

"Whoa," said Vern, punching the button on the digital recorder. "Slow up there a second, son. Let's talk. You've done some excellent research here. It's highly convincing stuff. It just needs a little more meat on the bones. People need to be able to imagine these places a little bit. You've got to get them using their imaginations a little bit."

Perry looked a little blank.

"Well, let's take San Marino. Like, how does it protect itself? Does it have an army?"

Perry shuffled through his papers. "It has a crossbow corps of eighty archers? But they just give demonstrations at festivals?"

"That's perfect," said Vern. "That would get people thinking. Say you didn't have to support a real army, the way we do now. Maybe just some ski-soldiers. That would free up some tax money. Okay, Luxembourg. What's weird about it?"

"Well, to graduate high school you have to be fluent in Luxembourgish, French, and German?" said Perry. "Also they have professional basketball, with a lot of guys who played college ball in America?"

"Okay, okay," said Vern. "We need a little more of that. Shall we give it another try?"

He punched the Record button, leaned into his microphone, and began. "Friends and neighbors, it's time for the next in our series of occasional broadcasts."

The pair worked for three hours, till the light in the room made it impossible to see outside. Vern turned off the bulb, and with only the glow of the laptop, the end of the day was visible again—a soft gray, with a streak of pink high up above the tree line. "I think it's pretty much a take," said Vern. "I don't know if you've sold everyone on a free Vermont, but I bet you'll convince a few folks to emigrate to Liechtenstein. Only the fun part left—are you ready for the anthem contest?"

Perry rummaged through his bag and pulled out an iPod, which he attached to the laptop with a cable and then thumbed through a list of songs, squinting to see the tiny screen. "Got it," he said.

"Friends and neighbors," said Vern, pushing the Record button once more, "we've subjected you to a good deal of information in this little broadcast—if you want the links, we'll stick them up on Radio Free Vermont. But before we go, something else new that we need your help with. Any nation needs a national anthem, so we're going to organize a little contest here. You can write your own, if you want, and send it in, and we'll play it on the air. Don't think 'I can't write an anthem'—think 'The United States of America made it two centuries with a terrible anthem that no one can sing. I bet I can do better than that.' But while we're waiting, we've got a few possibilities picked out for you too. My colleague Perry, besides his debating skills, is a virtual musical almanac, as long as that almanac is from the years 1960 to about 1978.

Which were pretty good years, anyone would admit. Anyway, Perry, what's your first contender?"

"Well, Vern," he said, sounding considerably more relaxed than when the afternoon had begun, "I thought it might be appropriate at least to listen to a song by the great Mavis Staples. She was born in 1939 in Chicago, Illinois, and she sang with her family in the Staples Singers. You know them from their number one hits 'Let's Do It Again' and 'Respect Yourself.' But Mavis sang solo too, and this is her first hit, from a Memphis recording session in the fall of 1969. I'm not sure it's an anthem, but it's the kind of song that—that makes you feel strong. Miss Mavis Staples, 'I Have Learned to Do Without You.'"

8

The three of them were sitting around the kitchen table that night, deep in conversation about the small nations of the world (Brunei, population 436,620; Iceland, 335,878). "Malta has only 415,196 people but it qualified for the finals of the Eurovision song contest every year from 1991 to 2006," Perry said. "And even then there was controversy—the computer may have counted Maltese votes for Greece."

"Is there really a falcon there?" asked Sylvia.

"What?" said Perry, but before anyone could explain, a headlight flashed through the curtains.

"Basement," hissed Sylvia, putting the two extra plates out of sight in the deep sink. Perry and Vern opened the door to the cellar and clambered down the stairs. Sylvia closed it behind them, just as the doorbell rang. She wiped her hands on a tea towel that hung from the oven door, pausing a second to collect herself, and then opened the door.

The woman on the other side was unfamiliar and at first glance undistinguished—middling height, middling-length brown hair, middling face. She looked up at Sylvia in the door and said, "Sorry to bother you. I'm looking for Vern."

"Who?" asked Sylvia.

"Vern Barclay," she said. "His mother said I'd find him here."

"I don't know a Mr. Barclay—maybe he was a friend of my ex-husband's?" asked Sylvia.

"Maybe so," the woman agreed. "But if he happens to drop by, tell him Trance was looking for him."

"Trance?"

"Trance—and sorry to bother you."

The woman turned and walked back to her rusty Saab, flipped the headlights on, and drove slowly out along the long drive.

Sylvia was shaking as she closed the door and returned to the kitchen. She waited a few minutes before she opened the door to the cellar, and when the pair climbed back out, it was to a kitchen darkened save for one small lamp by the sink.

"What was that all about?" asked Vern.

"Let me ask you something first," said Sylvia. "You're supposed to be a fugitive, right? You're supposed to be a wanted terrorist, yes? And no one is supposed to be able to find you here because no one knows we're friends, right?"

"Yes," said Vern a little uneasily.

"Well then, let me ask you one more question. Why did you tell your mother that you were in my house?" asked Sylvia, in a voice icy calm.

"That was my mother?" asked Vern. "My mother hasn't driven in five years."

"That was not your mother, though it would have been nice to send you home with her if it had been," said Sylvia. "That was someone your mother told your whereabouts to, which leads me, quick thinker that I am, to believe you may have told your mother first."

"Well," said Vern. "Yes. I mean, my mother is ninety-six. I couldn't just walk away without any explanation. So that first afternoon, while we were running, I stopped at a pay phone, of which there are damned few left, and gave her a call. But you don't know my mother—she's the toughest woman I ever met. She wouldn't tell a soul."

"Oh well, in that case never mind," said Sylvia. "Except why was there someone at my door asking for you, and the reason she was asking for you was because your mother had led her to believe you might be found here?"

"Uh, who was it?" asked Perry. "Like, was she the police?"

"That seems to me a reasonable guess," said Sylvia. "Which is why we'd better be thinking about where we're going, like, right now."

"We?" asked Vern.

"You don't think I'm going to let Perry abscond with a

fugitive who doesn't know not to tell his mother his hideout, do you?" said Sylvia. "Anyway, I'd say there's a pretty good chance they've got me in their card file now, wouldn't you?"

"She didn't say who she was?" asked Vern. "I mean, wouldn't the police have actually stuck around and looked for us?"

"Based on my extensive watching of TV, they're probably waiting for a warrant," said Sylvia. "Which should take about as long as, oh, a phone call. So maybe we better be going."

She was pulling a wedge of cheese and some yogurt out of the fridge and pushing them in a bag when Vern asked again. "She didn't say anything about who she was? Usually cops like to tell you they're cops."

"Only that her name was 'Trance,'" said Sylvia. "Which doesn't even sound real."

"Trance?" asked Vern, suddenly beaming and sitting back down. "Trance Harper? She was five-feet-six, a hundred thirty pounds, pure muscle?"

"She was wearing a coat and I don't guess weights at the Addison County Field Days," said Sylvia. "But that sounds about right. This is some friend of yours?"

"Trance Harper," said Vern. "You really don't remember Trance Harper? Perry, where's that computer? Can you get some video: 2006 Olympics, women's biathlon, Trance Harper."

Perry googled for a minute, till an image flickered on his screen. He held up the laptop, pressed a button, and instantly the image appeared on the flat-screen in the living room, which connected to the kitchen. Perry and Vern settled down on a couch, and Sylvia, still rattled, perched lightly on the arm, the bag of food still dangling from her grip.

The screen showed figure skaters, a Russian couple in white with sequins, sweeping around the rink to Igor Stravinsky's *Firebird*. After a few seconds, though, the voice of announcer Scotty Hamilton broke in. "We don't usually leave the skating rink during our prime-time coverage, even on an exhibition evening like this when the skaters are just putting on a show. But we have word of some drama up on the biathlon course, and so we're connecting you to our John Morton. Don't worry, we'll be back in the rink before Sasha Cohen debuts her new free program."

The picture shifted to two women in Lycra, both on skis, gliding to a halt and then pulling rifles from slings on their backs as they dropped nearly in unison to the ground, lying flat on their stomachs as they sighted the guns. "We're bringing you these pictures live because there's the chance here for something we've never seen before—an American medal in biathlon," the commentator was saying. "That's young Trance Harper there on the ground, next to the veteran German star Uschi Disl. This is their fourth and last shooting stage, and Harper has shot clean—hit all five targets—in each of the three previous rounds. If she cleans again here, then it's a full-on race to the finish with Disl, the best biathlete in the world."

The two guns cracked almost simultaneously, and the screen flashed a pair of hits on the first targets. "This sport is so tough because you have to do two exactly opposite things," the commentator was saying. "These girls have been skiing at top speed for the last five kilometers, but when they shoot they've got to drop their heart rates enough that there's a chance to squeeze off a bull's-eye. It's like trying to drink a quart of whiskey and fill out your tax returns at the same time, or run up a flight of stairs and thread a needle at the top." Two more sharp reports, two more clean hits.

"Trance Harper—her real name is Ellen, but they call her Trance for the way she focuses when she's on course—comes from rural Vermont." *Bang, bang.* "Two more hits, these girls are as evenly matched as you can imagine. You haven't heard of her because biathlon is about the most minor sport in the American pantheon, and she's in her first Olympics at the age of twenty-six, a late bloomer. She's only had a few races at the World Cup level." *Bang,* and Harper's target fell. A split second later, the German's gun fired, and another bull's-eye. "Only one target left for each, and if they hit them, then it's a drag race to the finish, one more lap around this five-kilometer course," the announcer said. "If either one misses, it's a hundred-meter penalty loop before they leave the range and they can kiss the gold goodbye. You can see some other competitors coming into the range now, but they're racing for the bronze. This pressure is too much—the hopes of the whole American skiing community riding on her here."

The camera zoomed in close on Trance, lying in the snow, sweat on her brow. "That's her, by the way," said Sylvia, who had put down the cheese and yogurt and now sat cross-legged on the floor.

The tip of the American's gun wavered from side to side. Next to her, a little out of focus, the German fired, and hit— she clambered to her feet, but Harper didn't seem to notice. She steadied herself, squeezed the trigger, and leaped up with a pump of her fist as the target fell. "She did it," screamed the announcer. "She's up and skiing—about five seconds behind Disl leaving the range, with maybe fifteen minutes of racing to catch her."

They watched as the pair sprinted out of the range and into the pine-lined course, a gentle snow falling. "What happens?" said Sylvia. "Does she win?"

Vern didn't say a thing—he was as reluctant to jinx it as he had been that afternoon in Turin, when he couldn't bear to watch the live video feed in the finish stadium where he waited. There was no way to explain to these two how impossible the moment was: an American actually threatening to best the Norwegians and the Swedes and the Germans. And not just any American, but Trance.

"Sometimes there's a little cat-and-mouse in these situations," said the broadcaster. "But not here. Disl has been the fastest skier on the World Cup circuit for the last three seasons, and she's determined to ski away from the American, to shut her down. But Harper doesn't seem to have gotten the memo—she's right on her skis."

"Those hills are so much steeper than they look," said

Vern, as the pair skittered up an incline. "That's a mountain they're climbing, at full speed. It hurts just to watch."

"Like many biathletes, Harper is part of the National Guard," the announcer was saying. "When the Olympics is done, she's due for a deployment in the Middle East. But right now all she's thinking about is that finish line, less than a kilometer away." The two broke out of the woods, and into the stadium, past bleachers lined with flag-waving spectators. Dead even now, they circled a curve and then headed the last two hundred meters for home, pushing with each stride. "I think she's doing it," the announcer screamed, and indeed each push seemed to carry Trance an inch or two farther than the German. She crossed the finish line maybe a foot in front, and crumpled in a heap, with Disl on the snow beside her, gasping for breath. Her teammates poured over the barriers at the edge of the course, and picked her up, unclipping her from the skis, hugging her, a scene of such jubilation that the announcer said not a word, just let the cameras take it in. Harper hugged the German, high-fived her coach, and then trotted toward the edge of the course, looking left and right for someone. When she found him she jumped into his arms, and the camera panned in on a shot of a beaming Vern, before breaking away to show a replay of the finish.

"Uh, that's you?" said Perry. "What were you doing there?"

"Quiet," said Vern. "This is the best part." The camera crew had caught up with Trance, still panting, a little film of spittle glistening on her chin. "How does it feel to be the first

American, man or woman, ever to win a biathlon medal, and a gold at that?"

"Um, good," she said.

"I love that," said Vern. "Like, that right there's the only possible answer. It feels good. I think that was the moment Vermont really fell in love with her. She was the Calvin Coolidge of sports. No thanking-her-lord-and-personal-savior, no I'm-going-to-Disney-World. Just 'good.'"

"We're going back to the rink now, and a night of figure skating," the commentator was saying. The video ended, and Perry thumbed the screen to sleep; the room darkened.

"Okay, I kind of remember her. I mean, I pay no attention to sports at all, except of course the racing at Thunder Road, but I remember seeing that answer over and over. Didn't they use it in a milk commercial?"

"That's it," said Vern. "Booth Brothers Dairy—'Um, good.'"

"But what were you doing there?" Perry asked again.

"Well, when I was young, as I said in that podcast the other day, I was a pretty good biathlete. Not quite good enough, but close. So later, when I was working in radio, I'd coach kids. Just beginners, just on the weekends. Teach them how to ski, show them how to shoot. As soon as they got good, they'd go into a real program with real coaches, but over the years I found a few prospects. No one like Trance, though. She was determined the first time I ever saw her, eight years old, and she just got tougher. Physically, but mentally too."

"You were the first person she went looking for," said Sylvia.

"Trance didn't have the easiest time of it," said Vern. "Her father was a drunk who left. Her mother is a saint—Estelle—but Trance has six brothers and sisters. There wasn't a lot of time and money. Fran and I made sure that she had equipment and could afford to travel. She was just a little younger than our kids, and she spent lots of time at our house. Fran was too sick to travel when the Olympics came around, but she made me go. Glad I did."

The house was quiet, breathing slowly. The tension from the knock on the door, and the tension of watching Trance win the race, had drained away. "I wonder what she wanted here," said Sylvia. "And I wonder if she'll come back."

"Don't know about the first," said Vern. "But as to the second, I don't imagine she'll be long. As I say, determined."

"Actually, Coach," said a voice from behind the sofa, "I've been here a couple of minutes already."

9

"How did you get in here?" said Sylvia, with some steam in her voice.

"How are you?" asked Vern, reaching for a hug.

"Good," said Trance, returning the embrace, and then she turned to face Sylvia. "I'm sorry. I figured if I knocked on the door again we'd go through the same routine, and since I could see you all through the window that seemed—bad."

"You were looking through the windows?" said Sylvia.

"I was, the same one I just climbed in. I haven't seen that race in years."

"You were good," said Perry.

"Trance—this is Perry Alterson. From Burlington. He knows computers," said Vern. "And this is Sylvia Granger, known mostly as Syl, who owns this house that the three of us have in one way or another invaded."

"I really am sorry, and I'll leave if you want," said Trance.

"Not before you tell us how you knew we were here."

"Oh. Well, like I said, I asked Vern's mother, Rose."

"And she just told you, 'My fugitive son is hiding out at 454 Route 28A in Starksboro'?"

"More or less. She said, 'I wouldn't tell anyone else, but I know Vern would want me to tell you,' and then she did."

"Well, that's pretty airtight security," said Sylvia.

"You've never met Rose, right?" asked Trance. "Because otherwise you'd know she's tough. I don't mean 'She's tough for being ninety-six.' I mean, if she hadn't wanted me to find out, I wouldn't have found out. Anyway, she had something she wanted delivered."

She loosened one strap on the rucksack that she was carrying, rummaged through a bit, and pulled out a neatly folded triangle of white cloth. "She made it with the other sewing ladies at the home," said Trance.

Vern reached out and took the cloth, untucking the edge of the triangle and unfolding it neatly. It was a flag, full-sized, grommeted, ready to raise. On a field of snowy white, the unmistakable silhouette of Camel's Hump mountain rose in forest green. And that was all, save for the red letters across the top: THE GODS OF THE VALLEYS ARE NOT THE GODS OF THE HILLS.

"Wow," said Sylvia.

"Wow," said Perry. "But what's it mean?"

"You don't recognize that?" said Vern. "I keep forgetting

that grade school has changed a little since my time. That's Ethan Allen. But the story may take a moment, and perhaps a bottle of beer?"

Sylvia warmed some dinner for Trance, and poured everyone a glass of Hogback Mountain Brewery's Railroad Hefeweizen. "Our nearest brewery," she said. "The house beer."

"Cheers," said Trance, who had taken off her jacket. She wore a tracksuit, and it was clear that though Vern hadn't seen her for a while, solid muscle was still the rule. "I'm sorry again," she said to Sylvia. "It wasn't very polite. And this soup is good."

"Not a problem," said Sylvia quietly. "There's plenty more soup."

"Here's what you need to know about Ethan Allen," said Vern. "He was a remarkable man, but he wasn't exactly a patriot in the Washington mold. He was a common man. Like a lot of other people, he'd bought a piece of land in Vermont— the colonial governor in New Hampshire was making himself a lot of money selling titles. The trouble was, the colonial governor of New York thought everything east of the Connecticut River belonged to him. And he had enough pull to get the king to agree. So the New Hampshire grants were ruled invalid, and New York started reselling the land to speculators.

"Ethan Allen went to Albany for the great court battle, but it was a put-up job. The judges were puppets; they held that all the people farming Vermont had to buy their land again, this time from the New Yorkers. The next day the attorney general of New York visited with Allen, and told him to go tell his friends to make the best terms they could with their new landlords. His advice came with a veiled apology and a veiled threat: "Might often prevails over right," he pointed out, with the confidence you'd expect from a representative of the mightiest empire on earth. Ethan Allen looked at him and said, 'The gods of the valleys are not the gods of the hills, and you shall understand it.' And he headed home.

"When he got there, he assembled the Green Mountain Boys—remember, these were men faced with losing their land. And they passed a resolution. I'm quoting from memory here, resolving to protect their land from the New Yorkers 'by force, as law and justice were denied them.'"

"So is that us?" Sylvia asked. "By force?"

"Not too likely," said Vern. "I mean, I'm an NRA guy since my first deer rifle, and Trance can shoot better than anyone in the state, but something tells me we're likely to be outgunned. Old Ethan could pretty much fight the New Yorkers even up, and once he'd stolen that one cannon, it was enough to force the British out of Boston. He didn't have to worry about, oh, I don't know, *helicopters*. Or Predator drones. Some lieutenant sitting in the Nevada desert could put a missile down our chimney with a joystick, and then go coach afternoon practice for his daughter's soccer team. And anyway, our chief strength is that people kind of like us. They think we're sort of funny, and maybe even a little noble. And I imagine that would end right about the moment we shot someone."

"My chimney was just relined," said Syl. "It cost a fortune."

"I've got an idea," said Trance.

10

Vern and Trance were wandering the woods behind the farmhouse—a security risk, as Sylvia had pointed out, but as Vern had pointed out in turn, there were risks that went with cabin fever too. They'd struck straight for the small creek that paralleled the driveway, and followed it into a grove of birch and beech, the smooth-skinned bark of the latter pocked and pustuled with the disease that had spread across the Northeast these last decades.

"Are you sure you want to do this?" Vern asked.

"Yep," said Trance, who wore her warm-up jacket and sneakers.

"I mean, you're about the most iconic Vermonter there is—everyone except Sylvia knows Trance Harper. You know you'd need to go underground with us. Your life would change."

"My life changed already."

"You never really did tell me about Iraq."

"There's not so much to tell. I was in the Guard, and they sent me three times in five years, and then a tour to Afghanistan. It kind of took care of the rest of my twenties."

They sat for a minute on an old stone wall, now winding through what looked like primeval forest of shaggy yellow birches. But the ground was pretty flat, and walls don't get there by themselves; without even thinking, both of them knew this was old sheep meadow, from the days a hundred and fifty years ago when the state had been one large pasture, stretching much higher up the sides of the mountains than this. Back before the Erie Canal had opened the West, and farmers' sons discovered what topsoil looked like, and Vermont began its long, slow slide. Back when Vermont had three sheep for every person.

"But what was it like?" said Vern, who knew it took some work to get Trance to talk about anything, much less this.

"You know I was a sharpshooter—the first girl, right?"

"The Guard made sure everyone knew—you were their poster girl."

"Those weren't biathlon rifles, Vern. Those were a whole different thing. You sat a mile away and you watched through the scope, and when you shot, it took three seconds for the hit. We weren't compensating for wind—we were compensating for the curve of the earth. I mean, far away."

"How much did it bother you?"

"Sometimes not much, when I knew I was shooting one of

their snipers—if you could see a gun, fair enough. Sometimes more, when we went after someone for 'political' reasons. They were the head of some clan we didn't like that week, or the enemy of someone we did like that week. Then you'd watch through the scope, and wait till the wife was on the other side of the room."

"We were all proud of everyone who went," Vern said.

"Yeah, well. We lost more KIA from Vermont than any other state, considering our size," said Trance. "Not too clear why, or for what. You know I was there when Gus died."

Vern knew—he'd been at the funeral, since Gus Robinson was another of the biathletes he'd coached; it was one of the last times he'd seen Trance. But he didn't say anything.

"Not there exactly," she said. "It was an IED—he was on the way back to the airport to head home. We'd had a party for him the night before. The point is, there was no point. Nothing we were doing there had anything to do with protecting any of this," she said, waving her hand at the skeletal forest. "It was way bigger than this. So big it didn't mean anything."

She handed him her warm-up jacket—he saw the logo from a junior team he'd coached her on twenty years before—and bent to tighten her sneakers. "I'm going for a run," she said.

"You're staying in shape?" he said.

"I'm staying in habit," she said with a small smile. "See you back."

Vern kept wandering. He'd spent enough time in the world's great landscapes to know this wasn't one of them. There weren't but a few acres of old-growth trees left in Vermont, and even they weren't especially grand—a few giant white pines, but nothing like a redwood. There were no seas of jagged granite peaks, no Class V whitewater cataracts. When the Audubon Society made calendars each year, eleven of the twelve pictures came from out West, with alpenglow and buck elk and wildflower meadows. Vermont supplied October, and it was usually a close-up of a maple leaf spinning in an eddy on some tiny stream.

Still, he thought as he meandered, he wouldn't trade. Not Vermont for Montana, not Big Sky for the filtered glimpses of blue and white through the treetops, not hardwood for high granite. For one thing, when that yellow came to Vermont, and the red and the orange with it, the colors kept you nearly giddy. These last few years had been drab by comparison with the past—summers too droughty, or so the weathermen said—but it was still a kind of explosion, with all of April's promise and August's heat building into a climax that came and went with surprising speed. The tour buses came from Boston for Columbus Day weekend, but that was always four or five days too late—the color still sharp, but subsiding.

And when it was over, it was even better. The leaves were down by mid-October, and you could see the shape of the land again, see the late sun silhouetting the trees along the ridgetops as it set. You could sense the architecture of the hills, every hollow and creekrun and knoll visible from the road. When people thought of trees, they thought of leaves—that's how a child would draw them. But the natural inclination of trees at this latitude was bareness—seven months of the year, at least upslope, they stood there stoic. Leaves were the fever-dream exception to the barren rule, and Vern felt calmer once they were down.

He hiked on, watching for the open seeps in what should have been an icy wood. Out West when you walked you looked up—the mountains were mostly open, you could see for miles, hundreds of miles. But Vermont was closed in now that the sheep were gone, more than four-fifths forest. You couldn't normally see a hundred feet in any direction, and so you tended to look down. And so the glories were minor key:

The splay of turkey tail fungus on a downed stump

The root of a birch arched high across a rock

A healthy pile of moose droppings, just smaller than Ping-Pong balls

Vern contemplated that last for a moment. You didn't see moose very often—you didn't see much wildlife, because the woods were dense, and it was easy for anything shy to disappear. He'd seen more deer in an afternoon at his sister's house in suburban Connecticut than in a season of sitting in his deer stand, rifle on his knees. (His brother-in-law would circle the house after dark, peeing on the shrubbery to keep the does away.) He remembered a trip to Yellowstone when the kids were young, and how odd it had seemed to be able to stand on a ridge and *see* bears and elk and bison wandering by below, in full view. He felt embarrassed for them; it seemed much more natural just to come across traces: scat, or a buck rub on the soft bark of a cedar, or the claw marks of a bear after beechnuts. He didn't need to see the animal itself, any more than he needed to see his neighbors in their houses when he drove down the road—the thin line of smoke coming up from the chimney was assurance enough.

But knowing that moose had returned to Vermont in his lifetime pleased him enormously. It was the idea that things repaired themselves, that if you backed off a little and didn't ask too much of the world then it would meet you halfway. This was one of the few corners of the planet that had gotten *better* in the last century, he thought—greener, healthier. The damage that too many sheep had done was wearing off. Or maybe you didn't even need to think of it as damage. It had been good then, when Vermont was full of farmers, and it was good now, when Vermont was full of trees.

Life ebbed and flowed, came and went. Goodness didn't demand the one-way arrow toward Progress and More. It was, he thought, a blessing to have lived out his life in a place that spun slowly like that yellow leaf, an eddy in the American rapids, a place that was shrinking when most of the country was growing growing ever-growing. A place where—*yow*, a place where a grouse might fire up at any moment from right under your legs, scaring the wits out of you as it somehow flew off at top speed between the tangle of trunks and branches.

A place where moss covered the back of a giant boulder, what the geologists delightfully called an "erratic" dropped in place when the last glaciers melted away.

A place where the beech leaves still clung brown to the branches, shaking a little in the too-warm breeze.

That too-warm breeze pulled Vern out of his contentment. He saw a sloppy pile of bear scat on the ground next to his foot, and he shook his head—bears were not supposed to be out in the woods in January, not in Vermont. They should be in their dens. Vermont might be a place outside the world's rush, but the world's rush was doing it in—winter was vanishing, a fact that he connected to that Walmart, and to that larger globe it in turn was linked to. You couldn't just ignore the world, that was the problem, because now it pressed in on you, without regard for borders. Most presidents in his lifetime you could forget for weeks at a time, but not this one, with the endless twittering. Too much somewhere else became too much here.

Which was why he was a fugitive, he supposed—why he was hiding fifty feet back from the edge of the woods, unseen but able to watch Sylvia's class hard at work in the driveway. They were learning to run a fire truck, an older pumper like the one most volunteer companies could afford in the small towns. This one was a beauty—Sylvia used it in parades, with a sign for her school bolted to the side. But like all fire equipment, it was basically a pump on wheels, and pumps are always trouble, as Vern knew from many years of Saturday-morning fire company meetings dominated by topics like "The Gasket Dried Out" and "It Won't Hold a Prime."

At the moment, a former investment banker and a retired radiologist were standing on the bridge behind the truck's cab, pointing at a dial and arguing. Vern couldn't hear them, but he knew what they were discussing: had the pressure risen high enough to open the nozzle? Sylvia jumped up next to them, yelled something, and they flipped the valve for the deck gun, which immediately started spraying a long and stately arc into the woods. It was as if she knew just where he was standing—suddenly there was a rainstorm erupting all around him. Moving quickly, he crossed to a small grove of hemlock, which caught most of the falling water in its needles. As he looked up, he was startled to see Trance standing there grinning at him.

"How'd you find me?" he asked. "You've been running two hours."

"And you've covered about two hundred yards," she said.

"I've covered a lot of ground in my mind, though," he said. "I'm reasonably sure we're on the right track. Or at least that we're supposed to be doing *something*, not just letting the world walk itself straight to hell."

"Or someplace of a similar temperature," said Trance. "It's too hot."

"Well, maybe for the best today if they've got the hoses going," Vern said, peering out through the forest at the fire truck, its thousand-gallon tank spent in less than a minute of wild white spray.

"They're having fun because they have helmets," said Trance. "Guys like dressing up."

"Yes they do," he said, remembering the pleasure of climbing into his turnout gear whenever there was a chimney fire to put out somewhere in town. You needed to keep the cuffs of the pants tucked into the top of the boots so you could jump right in. The heavy coat and the suspenders always made you feel a bit like a boy pretending to fight a fire, even when you had a real hose in your hand.

"Here's your jacket," he added, handing her the warm-ups he'd been holding for two hours. "Let's get you inside before you chill."

11

"Oh my, the governor is looking pleased with himself," said Vern. He and Perry were sprawled on the couch in front of Sylvia's TV. They were watching Vermont's only television station, WVTV, which today was offering live coverage of an event that even now the governor was calling "the apex and the apogee of what we've worked for here in Vermont all these years.

"People always call us 'tiny Vermont,'" he continued. "No one likes to be called small; it is demeaning—I remember agreeing when Mr. Trump, during his campaign, reacted strongly to the idea that his fingers were somehow smaller than ordinary. So during my administration we have concentrated on growth, on expansion, on making sure that we can stand erect and proud. We have passed North Dakota in population, and we remain well ahead of Wyoming. And beginning today we have a World Class Facility to showcase our state's World Class Quality of Life." Governor Bruce was able to speak in capital letters—each word got its own puff of breath. He was beaming as he gestured.

"He's standing on a wooden box behind that lectern," said Vern. "He's been using it since he ran for class president at UVM." Vern had told the others Bruce's history over breakfast—it overlapped with his own, since he'd known the governor's older sister since grade school. Some of Leslie's fixation on size may have stemmed from his five-foot-four frame, Vern maintained, but he conceded that if so, it had only fueled his prodigious work ethic. He'd gained the corner office in Montpelier by shaking more hands and cutting more ribbons than any politician in history—and since Vermont really *was* a small state, that counted for a good deal. "We used to say that if you forgot to rent a clown for your kid's birthday party, you could just call up the governor's office and he'd come make balloon animals for you." Once installed in office, he'd stayed there by making sure that the state's few big industries—the semiconductor plant in particular—got every break they needed; in return, they made sure he got every campaign contribution he required. By contrast with the man in Washington, he wasn't bizarre or even creepy, just standard-issue hack. His main sin, in Vern's eyes, was that he'd done nothing to arrest Vermont's slow slide into facelessness. The governor's credo was simple: no new taxes ever. Unless it was designed to build something Big.

And nothing was bigger than the building looming up behind him on the TV screen as he spoke. "The Good People of our Great State have never had a suitable place in which to gather," he said. "Our largest arenas held only a few thousand people. But today we inaugurate this facility, with its capacity of twenty-eight thousand people—twenty-eight thousand Vermonters. And as you all know, it comes with a Retractable Roof."

"He's been talking about the retractable roof for ten years," said Vern. "He'd come on my show and just say it, over and over again." Perry shushed him—the governor had paused dramatically, but now was continuing.

". . . humbles me to say that the state commission on historic sites—and this is a Historic Site even before its opening—informed me today that it would be named the Governor Leslie R. Bruce World Class Facility. As a reserved New Englander, that embarrasses me a little, but since they are an Independent Commission it would be wrong for me to block their work. In any event, what matters is that the State of Vermont now has a facility as large as the Times Union Center in Albany, or the Carrier Dome in Syracuse—and neither of those have a Retractable Roof. As a result, we will be able to attract National Caliber Acts to visit our state. In fact, today I can announce that I have worked with the state's arts director to secure the inaugural season of performances, drawing on some of my very favorite artists. You will be pleased to know that . . . Nickelback will open this new Facility with a free concert, and that they will be joined by . . . Barry Gibb, the surviving member of the Bee Gees!"

"Nickelback," said Perry, stunned. "Are you kidding me? Are there whiter people in the entire universe. Oh my god. What's the matter? Was Foreigner already booked? Oh my god." The JumboTron on the façade of the new arena was suddenly pulsing "Nickelback, Nickelback, Nickelback," and Perry just groaned.

". . . also be ready to host trade shows and events from across the nation. Interstate commerce is the lifeblood of our great nation, and though it is regrettably true that we still have fewer big box stores than some of our peer states. Though I should add that the Saint Albans Walmart Supercenter will have its grand reopening on Tuesday. Anyway, we now have a Facility for holding conventions and exhibitions which will help Jumpstart the Economy by Showcasing our Talented Workforce. I can announce today that, thanks to the hard work of my commerce department, in early March we will host the thirty-fourth annual Leisure Furniture Showcase. Last year in Boca Raton, This Year in Burlington!"

"Leisure furniture?" said Vern. "That's definitely what we need more of."

The crowd of dignitaries clapped strenuously, and the governor beamed anew. "Because this is such a Signal Event for our state, I've asked one of our World Class Ambassadors to raise the flag that marks this inauguration. And not just any flag. This is the flag that flew at the Top of the Olympic Flagpole when Trance Harper won her Olympic Gold Medal in Biathlon. Trance, could you please raise the flag—and when it reaches the top of the pole, I will depress this lever, causing the Retractable Roof to open for the very first time."

"Gotta get ready to push my own button," said Perry, fiddling with the laptop on the coffee table in front of him.

"No rush, this will take a while," said Vern. And indeed, Trance had risen from her seat on the dais and was making her way not to the flagpole but to the lectern where the governor stood. He held his ground for a minute, but—no match for solid muscle—stood a step aside. Trance towered above the microphone, until she used her foot to push away the governor's wooden box. Then she reached into the pocket of her official warm-ups and pulled out a piece of paper, which she unfolded slowly.

"Governor Bruce and assembled dignitaries," she said. "I am honored to be here today. As I am not a gifted public speaker such as yourself"—the governor beamed, a little uncomfortably—"I have written down a few words to say on this occasion."

Actually, Vern (with the occasional interjection from Perry and Sylvia) had written most of them, though he hoped he'd done it in her voice, and he had his own copy on his knee so he could follow along.

"I grew up in Vermont," she said. "And it was always fine with me that it was a small state. My mother had a small business which produced a small income, but we had a large number of friends, many of whom helped raise me. I went to a small school, where I knew everyone and everyone knew me. They knew I didn't like to talk in public, so they didn't make me. I learned a small sport, where tiny details make all the difference, and I won the Olympic medal by the smallest of margins. And then I went away, like so many thousands of other Vermonters, to very big wars in a very big world. I do not regret my service, and I'm not ashamed of it; I'm proud of my brothers and sisters in the military. But I didn't feel as if I was protecting Vermont. I felt like I was protecting bigness— big oil and big companies who made big money running those wars. And when I got home, I saw more clearly that bigness coming to my state: not just big box stores, but big box houses built by people who'd made big money in big banks in big cities. And who drove very big vehicles, usually quite badly. Big dairies putting all the small farms I knew out of business. And the big problems it's all causing, not least of which is that we never have big snows anymore, which is big trouble if you're a skier."

Here she put aside the paper and looked straight at the governor. "Anyway, now we've got this big palace to dedicate.

"The first thing I want to say is that Nickelback really sucks and if you want some out-of-state music you should bring in"—and here she took another piece of paper out of her pocket and unfolded it—"the Staples Singers, to perform

'If You're Ready Come Go with Me,' which peaked at number nine on the pop charts in 1973."

"Yes!" said Perry.

"And the other thing is, Governor, I decided to bring a different flag with me for the dedication, this one even more special than my Stars and Stripes from the Olympics. This one was sewn by Mrs. Addison Barclay and friends at the Blake Avenue Home for Elder Women in Montpelier. If you want, you could call her the Betsy Ross of a Free Vermont." And with that she stepped to the flagpole, snapped the lanyards through the grommets in her flag, and hoisted it hand over hand, seven good pulls sufficing to reach the top.

As the flag unfurled, several things happened at once.

For one, the giant JumboTron stopped flashing "Nickelback" and started flashing, in quick sequence, "Size Matters," "The Gods of the Valley," "Are Not the Gods of the Mountains," "Drink Local Beer," and "Radio Free Vermont."

For another, Tommy Augustus, who had been watching with slowly dawning trepidation, started talking rapidly into a cell phone. "She's with Barclay. Get her!"

And for a third, the governor, who had long since stopped beaming, nonetheless carried on as if everything had happened according to plan. He stepped to the lectern and declared, "I will now Depress the Lever that will operate the only Retractable Roof in northern New England . . ." He'd lost his crowd, however—they were too busy pointing at the flag, and the scurrying policemen, and the JumboTron, which now was flashing "Good Things Come in Small Packages," and "I Voted for Leslie Bruce and All I Got" "Was This Monstrosity."

In the uproar, the state police managed to miss the five-foot-six woman in the USA warm-ups, who ducked beneath the temporary bleachers, trotted two blocks down a side street, and jumped onto the running board of a pumper truck. Someone tossed her a helmet and a coat, and they sirened off south down Route 7 unnoticed. Meanwhile, the roof ponderously retracted, opening the Gov. Leslie R. Bruce Facility to the warm winter air.

12

"Are there actually any white people whose music you appreciate?" Sylvia asked. They were discussing the events of the day before, which ended with the JumboTron flashing "Nickelback? Why Not Kenny Rogers?"

"Dusty Springfield?" said Perry. "Queen of blue-eyed soul? I mean, 'The Look of Love,' all by itself. But in 1970 she came to Tennessee to record *Dusty in Memphis*, one of *Rolling Stone*'s hundred best albums of all time. It's true that white people loved it—'Son of a Preacher Man' reached number ten on the Austrian charts, and number three in Switzerland. But she also brought the first Motown revue to England. And when she went to South Africa in 1964, her contract stipulated she'd only play to unsegregated audiences. It basically shut down the tour?"

"I liked that Staples song," said Trance. "Can you make me a mix for when I'm running?"

"You're not running anytime soon," said Vern. "You're a prisoner here for a while, with Perry and me. If there's anyone in Vermont the governor would like to see locked up this morning, it's you."

He was looking through the morning papers, which Syl had spread out on the dining room table. "BIG-Time?" the *Rutland Herald* asked. "Trance Rains on Governor's Parade— Right Through Retractable Roof." The *Burlington Free Press* had a picture of the Free Vermont flag flapping, with the giant building looming ominously out-of-focus in the background, and another of Vern's mother and six of her gray-haired friends holding a different version of the banner out on the steps of their retirement home.

"Aren't you worried we're going to get your mom in trouble?" Sylvia asked.

"I was more worried about what she'd do if I didn't give her credit," said Vern. "She'll love every moment of this. And even Leslie Bruce is not crazy enough to do anything to a ninety-six-year-old."

"Did you know your mom had a Facebook page?" said Perry. "She just updated it with the sewing pattern for the flag."

"Speaking of which, are we reaching the world?" Vern asked.

"Well, our site is shut down, of course, but it doesn't matter that much. People have cached everything important a hundred other places. And the YouTube of the flag is going viral—forty-eight hundred thousand views as of six a.m., and there's a version set to 'If You're Ready Come Go with Me.'"

"That means we've got work to do," said Vern, pouring a large cup of coffee. "Here's how the news cycle works. We're hot till something else happens, hotter still if they react. But the moment some pro wrestler conceives a child with a politician's daughter, then we're out of the news. We might as well make hay while the sun shines, as my haymaking father used to say. And since we can't exactly call a press conference, that means back up to the studio. How many people listened to the last podcast?"

"Sixty thousand downloads," said Perry.

"This will be six hundred thousand, thanks to Trance. So I guess it better be good," Vern replied, cracking his knuckles with pleasure.

"Just like your radio show, isn't it?" said Sylvia. "But no yells of triumph when you're done. My class arrives in an hour, and we'll be indoors today, down in the basement. And hopefully we'll be very quiet. Trance, you'll need to make yourself scarce. But if you're interested, you can sit in the laundry room and listen—just keep the door locked."

Perry and Vern trooped upstairs, settling into the pair of chairs on the braided rug arrayed in front of the microphone and laptop. "I don't really need the headphones, but I feel easier with them on after all these years," said Vern, covering his right ear with one pad and letting the other rest just behind his left, so he could still hear Perry. "It won't take much to get me started today, but fire me a question or two that have come in—and I take it you've got some music ready for the outro?"

"Of course," said Perry. "And here's a question that I've been thinking about too. It comes from Dana in Hartland—where's Hartland?"

"Over on the Connecticut, near Dartmouth," said Vern. "Read it into the microphone."

"'Dear Mr. Barclay—The last time anyone tried to secede, my great-grandfather went down to Tennessee and got killed at the Battle of Chickamauga. There's a monument in our town to all the men who died "to preserve the Union." Were they wrong to do it?'"

Vern settled forward, elbows on his knees, chin resting on his laced fingers, eyes closed, mouth a few inches from the mike. He paused just a second, and then began:

"Dana, thanks for that question. Let's make it the frame for broadcast number seven from Radio Free Vermont, underground, underfoot, and underpowered. We're brought to you today by Hill Farmstead's revelatory Abner IPA, a beer from the backroads of Greensboro Bend brewed for those warm days of . . . January. Sorry about the weather, folks, but you have to admit it made for a great show outside Bruce Stadium yesterday. And I hope you've pulled out your favorite Nickelback long-playing records to get ready for the big show!

"Now, to the excellent question from the Upper Valley.

Dana, a confession first. If there's a single place in the United States of America guaranteed to make me weep, it's the Lincoln Memorial. I can't look up at that sad, wise face and keep my composure, nor read the Second Inaugural etched on those stone walls. The president gave that speech after a week of rain—the dirt roads of the national capital were a sea of mud. And he spoke while the war still raged—things looked good for the North, but the South had not surrendered; he could have brayed for blood and vengeance, or boasted about 'Mission Accomplished,' but he did neither. If I recollect, he finished with these words: 'With malice toward none, with charity for all, with firmness in the right as God gives us to see the right, let us strive on to finish the work we are in, to bind up the nation's wounds, to care for him who shall have borne the battle and for his widow and his orphan, to do all which may achieve and cherish a just and lasting peace among ourselves and with all nations.' And a month later he was dead at the feet of the coward Booth." Here Vern paused, rocked back for a moment, then reset his chin on his knuckles.

"If you wanted to explain why Lincoln fought so hard to preserve the Union, the main reason of course is obvious. South Carolina and her Confederate sisters left the republic because they wished to continue the practice of owning slaves—wished to continue, as Lincoln put it in that inaugural, 'wringing their bread from the sweat of other men's faces.' The Vermonters who marched off to fight in that war—a higher percentage than in any other state—did so singing 'John Brown's Body.' They did so intending once and for all to end that odious practice. And no wonder. In 1777, while still an independent republic, Vermont became the first sovereign state on earth to constitutionally outlaw slavery; admitted to the Union in 1791, it was the first American state to do the same. In 1843, when Frederick Douglass toured our state, the legislature passed an ordinance forbidding sheriffs, bailiffs, jailers, constables, and citizens from detaining fugitives.

"And it was not just brave words—our cemeteries each November still sprout thousands of flags by the graves of those who died in the cause. Thirty-five hundred Vermonters entered the Battle of the Wilderness in Orange County, Virginia, in May of 1864, and 1,234 never returned. And an aside: a few years ago Walmart tried to build a store in the middle of that battlefield.

"But Dana—while slavery alone would be sufficient reason for Lincoln to have fought for Union, there was another cause as well. And it helps us understand the gulf between his time and our own. Remember the U.S. of Lincoln's day—a population of thirty million, already ten times larger than at the Revolution, but ten times smaller than our total today. Eighty percent lived in the countryside, but most of the countryside was as yet uninhabited, at least by Europeans. There was a great national project at hand, the project of settling a continent, and it needed the power of a central state to make it happen—to build the railroads that linked the oceans, to divide the land the homesteaders would settle, even to build the land grant colleges that would make America the most democratically educated place on earth. It was a Vermonter, Justin Smith Morrill, who introduced that bill, and Lincoln who signed it.

"I'm not saying that the spread West was all good. It came with many curses. Rutland's John Deere invented the 'plow that broke the plains'—and washed half the topsoil of a continent down the Mississippi. As the riches of the prairies were exposed, the Indians were routed and killed; the bison hunted near to extinction. It was not all good—but it was probably inevitable. The riches of those fields and forests and mines were going to be gotten, and the very bigness of the government made that project easier and fairer than it would otherwise have been. It's no accident that the first road across the country was called the Lincoln Highway.

"But now—now we have no such project. Lincoln's dream of a continent united sea to sea has long since been realized. We needed to be big to fight the Nazis—but fighting terrorists is much easier if we're quick and nimble. We needed to be big to send a rocket to the moon—but we've been there, done that. Now—maybe now we need to be small, or at least smaller. It's not like we can or should go off on our own—this Internet thing seems to ensure we'll always be in easy touch. But maybe we can trade recipes, not food. Maybe instead of oil in a giant ship from ten thousand miles away, we need sunlight on a small bank of panels on the roof. Maybe after a few hundred years of growing steadily bigger we're now big enough—now that our adolescence is over and it's time for our hormones to recede and bittersweet maturity to finally come. I want to leave you with something else Lincoln said, words that should be as famous as the Gettysburg Address. They came when he launched the Department of Agriculture, now a gross supplier of subsidy to corporate agribusiness. But that was not Lincoln's vision. Instead, he said—and here, friends, I can't pretend to remember, I must look at the notes I took yesterday, while I was waiting for our friend Trance to raise my mother's flag. Lincoln said that cultivating even 'the smallest quantity' of ground bred freedom and independence. 'Ere long the most valuable of all arts, will be the art of deriving a comfortable subsistence from the smallest area of soil. No community whose every member possesses this art, can ever be the victim of oppression of any of its forms. Such community will be alike independent of crowned-kings, money-kings, and land-kings.'

"We would like very much to be independent of kings, even kings with retractable roofs. And so we should think about going our own way—about standing on our own feet. We still have soil, and we still have people who know how to farm—and how to do a lot of other things as well. My guess is, Vermont on its own will be a lot closer to what Lincoln had in mind for a healthy country. And so, Dana, even once Vermont has won its independence, I hope you'll join me in keeping the celebration of Mr. Lincoln's birth—the twelfth of February approaches. And with it I note that the Thetford

League of Women Voters will be holding a bean supper that night. Congratulations to the St. Johnsbury Academy girls for that double overtime win at Burr and Burton last night, and good luck to the Catamounts as they take to the ice against Boston University tonight. Perry, do we have a song for Lincoln?"

"We have a song *by* Lincoln—Abbey Lincoln? It's 'Freedom Day,' from the album *We Insist* that she recorded with Max Roach in 1960." He pushed a button on his laptop, and the hard bop poured out through the speakers, her voice riding the notes. The two listened right through the song, Vern a little dazed. "That was harder than I meant to go," he said. "It wasn't really radio. It was more like a speech. But if we're going to get them, this is the moment." He straightened and stood and walked to the sofa against the window, where he lay down and closed his eyes.

13

The laundry room offered all the standard charms: slight mildew, lint fuzz, ancient linoleum. But there was a plastic lawn chair, and Trance sat in it, quietly folding a load of clothes and listening to the slightly muffled sounds coming from the basement room next door.

"You may wonder why we're spending the day indoors on folding chairs," Sylvia was saying to her assembled class. "I'm aware it's not as much fun as running the fire truck or sawing down trees or driving in the mud. We'll be back outdoors next time, practicing how to haul your neighbor's truck out of a ditch, or a snowbank if we ever get any snow again. But today is one of the most important lessons we have, and one of the hardest."

Trance could hear the squeak of chalk on board, and surmised that Sylvia had turned to the blackboard. "The first

Tuesday in March—can anyone tell me why that's an important day on the calendar?"

"NCAA basketball?" ventured one man.

"The Oscars?"

"No. The first Tuesday in March is the traditional time for town meeting. In Vermont, government begins at home. People gather on uncomfortable metal folding chairs exactly like the ones you currently inhabit. They spend all day discussing whether or not to build a new soccer field, if it's time to buy a new grader for the road, how much the town clerk should be paid. This is a democratic heritage that dates back to the Greeks, and as newcomers to Vermont, you will have a crucial role to play. Can anyone guess?"

No one answered, and after a minute Sylvia said:

"That is absolutely right. Your job is to stay silent. Not to say anything. After two or three years it is appropriate to congratulate the road superintendent for the good plowing work that winter. But if you want to fit in, your basic job is to shut up.

"This will be hard work," she continued. "For instance, what if I propose a resolution to raise the tax rate for a year in order to buy a rebuilt pumper truck."

"That's dumb," came a voice almost immediately. "It would be cheaper to pass a bond and pay for it over two decades—you'd be paying in 2030 money."

"Maybe so. But you wouldn't be paying it—your kids would," Sylvia said. "You will notice a Yankee aversion to debt that you may find quaint. But when the economy tanked in 2009, not one Vermont bank went under. There weren't thousands of homes built on spec. Let's keep going. Now I'm going to propose a tax increase to put a new roof on the school, even though it's only got twelve students in the incoming kindergarten class."

"That sounds like my new town," said one man. "It's ridiculous. It's time to consolidate with the next town over."

"Maybe—it would be more efficient," said Sylvia. "But you need to remember that the school is the center of a town. People went there, their kids went there. Sticking them on a bus is a hard decision. And small schools are good schools— if you have a private school somewhere, the classes are small. You guys can afford to pay more taxes—don't complain. But by the same token, for some people an increase in the tax rate is tough news—it means they have to log off the twenty acres of land they own. So don't be too quick to demand that the town build a swimming pool like the one you had back in Westchester. The point is, don't be too quick to demand anything. These towns are all two hundred and forty years old, and they've lasted that long because people have figured out how to make them last. They're good at this. Don't be so sure that your version of reality is better because it's newer. Watch for a few years and see if your town changes you before you change your town. Now we will practice for a while."

For a solid ten minutes Trance heard nothing at all,

except toward the end, the sound of Sylvia climbing the base-ment steps, and then descending again, and then unwrapping tinfoil. "Any good town meeting comes with refreshments," she said. "No one will mind if you bake some cookies, even for your first one."

14

Sylvia got back from the store at dusk and shouted an all-clear—as she pulled down the blinds in the kitchen, the crew reconvened. "I think we may be on a roll," she said. "There's a big 'Trance for Governor' sign out by the entrance to the landfill."

"Sheesh," said Trance.

"And at the general store Dick says he's pulling non-Vermont beer off the shelf. Bud Light will remain, since no one makes a light beer in Vermont and he says his lady clientele demand a light beer or else they get big in the rear. Did you know that men get beer bellies but ladies get beer bottoms? That's what Dick says. Present company excepted, of course. He had the Trout River Rainbow Red Ale on sale, so I got some."

"That's from Springfield," said Vern. "That's good beer."

Perry flicked on the small TV that hung next to the kitchen

sink. A picture of Tommy Augustus filled the screen. *"We've got several solid leads on the whereabouts of Barclay and his associates, including Trance Harper,"* he was saying. *"Terrorism—the deliberate attack on private property—is very much a crime, and so is flag desecration."*

"I didn't desecrate the flag. I just put up a different one," said Trance.

"This is good—they're reacting," said Vern. "What we've got to hope is that they keep talking about it, so that it's not a one-day wonder. We need a movement to start building, and since we're in no position to organize it ourselves, we're going to have to hope they do it for us."

The anchor reported "brisk sales" of the free Nickelback tickets, but added "good seats remain," and then showed the latest publicity photos of Barry Gibb, squeezed uncomfortably into a white suit.

"Oh my god," said Sylvia. "It looks like someone put too much bleach in the Enterprise washing machine."

"Let's turn on the radio instead," said Vern. "It's six past the hour, which is when they switch to the local news on WVRT. It's about the only local thing left over there, but they're good reporters, and they're my friends."

". . . Fallout from yesterday's fireworks continue across the state. In Shrewsbury today, two local chapters of the Boy Scouts of America announced they were disbanding and re-forming as 'Ethan Allen Scouts.' Their new greeting is 'The gods of the valley are not the gods of the hills.' And in Clarendon, the local post

of the NRA announced that they'd named Trance Harper an honorary chapter commander. 'I think she's right—when government gets too big it wants to take away your guns,' said Avary Holback, chapter president. 'We need small government and long rifles. Also, of course, handguns.'"

"Check this out," said Perry. "Your mom's Facebook page is going nuts. She's linked it up to Eldernet, and now there's a contest around Vermont for which home can stitch the most flags. They're bulk-ordering the green cloth for the Camel's Hump."

". . . *interest in the independence movement is spreading outside the state as well,"* the radio reported. *"In Boston this afternoon, where the Catamounts beat the BU Terriers two to one on a late shorthanded tally, UVM goalie Chris Chambeau pulled one of the new flags from beneath his jersey and began circling the rink. This is the sound of the chant coming from the BU students: 'Ver-mont. Ver-mont, Ver-mont.'"*

"It's starting," said Vern. "It's starting to work."

15

That very night, in fact, some Wikipedia-wielding historian noticed that it was the 247th anniversary of the day in 1777 when Vermont declared its independence from Britain. Since he also happened to be the Dorset volunteer fire chief, not to mention well into his second four-pack of Fiddlehead's bracing Second Fiddle IPA, he sounded the siren on the top of the firehouse for several minutes, which would have annoyed all the men who answered the call if he hadn't had several four-packs in reserve. They had cell phones; before the deadline for the eleven p.m. news, half the towns on the western side of the state had sounded their alarms, and coverage on the late newscast from WVTV was enough to convince the Norwich, Vershire, and St. Johnsbury departments that they were missing out on the fun.

The next morning, five postmasters in Caledonia County arrived at work to find the American flag neatly folded in a regulation triangle on the front steps, and a Vermont banner flying from the pole. Four replaced the flag; the fifth called the local newspaper to take a shot, and by noon the picture was spread across the top of the *New York Times* website to illustrate a feature story titled "In Quaint Green Mountain Hamlets, a Push for Independence."

In early evening, two young men with a piece of rope set up a "Free Vermont Border Check" on the Addison side of the newly rebuilt Crown Point Bridge. As incoming cars with New York plates slowed to a halt, they handed each driver an apple and a flyer advising of "national customs and cultural sensitivities":

> Vermonters do not like having their pictures taken, but if you offer them a beer they will usually allow it.
>
> ~
>
> Skimpy clothing is *encouraged* in Vermont.
>
> ~
>
> Being a dick and/or asshole or acting like a New Yorker is *discouraged* in Vermont.

Before the day was out, Ben & Jerry's had announced a new flavor: Trancicle, made only with Vermont milk and maple syrup, and "bullets" of dark chocolate. The lid showed Ben and Jerry holding the new flag and a newly discovered quote from General Allen: *"Ever since I arrived to a state of manhood, I have felt a sincere passion for liberty—and ice cream with a high butterfat content!"*

Seven Days, the state's alternative newspaper, printed a page of oval portraits of great Vermonters, sized so readers could paste them over the presidents on their U.S. banknotes, "pending the adoption of our own currency." Particularly popular were, besides Calvin Coolidge, the actor Orson Bean (born Dallas Burrows in Burlington, 1928), singer Rudy Vallee (born Hubert Vallée, Island Pond, 1901), suffragette Clarina Howard Nichols (Townshend, 1810), and Fred Tuttle (born Fred Tuttle, Tunbridge, 1919). Less cherished, according to a count of random tills published by the newspaper: Chester Arthur (Fairfield, 1829) and Fred Pabst, whose "pioneering work as a ski resort developer in the Manchester area was apparently outweighed by the fact that his money came from the family's watery beer."

Buch Spieler Records in Montpelier, the last record store remaining in the state, reported a run on Staples Singers CDs, and issued an instant mixtape: "Soulful Sounds for an Independent State of Mind: the Perry Alterson Collection," with every song he'd mentioned in his podcasts, plus a special coda: The Scorpions version of "I'm in a Trance."

Vermont Public Radio put out a press release acknowledging that its switchboard had been overwhelmed with calls from listeners who thought it was "un-Vermontlike" to continue describing itself as a member station of National Public

Radio. "We will take no position on this controversy," the station said, adding, "but we encourage all sides in this dispute to pledge their support in our winter fund drive, which begins tomorrow."

Though Perry provided regular updates from the Web, the crew holed up in the Starksboro farmhouse missed firsthand glimpses of what was going on. Only Sylvia, trekking to Hinesburg daily for groceries, had a real sense of how they were dominating not just the news but the imagination of their neighbors. "I saw three bumper stickers on the way back today," she said. "Two said 'Barclay for Governor.' One said 'Barclay for Prime Minister.'"

"That will not make Leslie Bruce happy," said Vern. "And it's only a matter of time before they start to hit back, and hard. But right now we've got the momentum, and our problem is we can't do anything about it. We started all this, but without figuring out how we'd make it real. We don't just need sentiment—we need a plan."

"We could call on people to rise up?" said Perry. "We could play 'Get Up, Stand Up for Your Rights' by Bob Marley, or the Peter Tosh version or the Toots and the Maytals version, but really not the Tracy Chapman version, I don't think."

"Excellent song, and it makes me want something a little stronger than this Harpoon UFO, hoppy though it is," said Sylvia. "But my guess is Vern will say we don't really want people just rising up. Anyone who simply rises up would get shot down, and our campaign with them. But I keep thinking about my last class. Town meeting is only, what, five weeks away? Isn't there something we could do there?"

Vern looked at her and smiled. "I think you've figured it out," he said, after a few minutes. "I really do. And I think we need a new broadcast. I need the computer for a few minutes of research, but let's do this one from the kitchen. Trance, we'll need you to say a few words."

"I've already talked too much!"

"People will just want to know you're here, and carrying on the fight," he said. "You can read the hockey scores. And Perry, you can start it off with Mr. Marley."

The laptop and the microphone sat on the kitchen table, and Vern sat with his eyes closed, meditating. He felt a particular mix of pleasures—he was about to talk into a microphone, which he was very good at, with two women he admired on hand to watch. And an impressionable boy—he was showing off. And not just for them, he realized, but for his audience out there in . . . not radioland. Podcastland. It was the same place really that he'd been speaking to for decades. But in this case he wasn't just telling someone else's story. He was the teller, and he was the tale. And the tale right now was going well—though he felt some serious foreboding, for the moment the wave was still building, and he could ride it. He could push it higher. He had to remind himself that understatement worked best, that he couldn't get too hot. He was talking about small and modest and Vermont, and he had to be small and modest and Vermont.

"Are you asleep?" asked Trance. "Because I'm pretty close to it. I didn't work out today and I'm more tired than if I did."

"Don't go yet," said Vern, who wanted the moment to last, and the audience right here in the kitchen was part of the moment. He wanted to add: *I always watched to the last lap of every race you ever entered.* But to say that would be to let on that he was competing, that he was putting on a show.

He nodded to Perry, and suddenly the sound of the great Jamaican filled the little room. After the first chorus, Perry started to fade the music out, and the slightly richer, slightly deeper voice that Vern used for the radio began to roll right in.

"Hello, friends. This is Vern Barclay, with broadcast number eight from Radio Free Vermont, underground, underpowered, and underfoot. Tonight we're brought to you by the McNeill's Brewery of beautiful Brattleboro, producer of among other things the very fine Duck's Breath Ale that animates our time together this evening. I'm sitting here with my friends Trance Harper and Perry Alterson and others of our co-conspirators not yet known to the powers that be. We've watched with great interest and a small amount of pride in the last few days as you've begun to take matters into your own hands. You've concocted ways to spread the idea of a free Vermont that would never have occurred to us, though I believe that its namesake would prefer if Ben and Jerry's made their Trancicle flavor more of a mint–chocolate chip.

"This movement is finally started, but movements need somewhere to go. We're not in charge of this effort, but we have thought about it a good deal, and we do have a suggestion. Think ahead, fellow Vermonters, to the first Tuesday in March, and Town Meeting Day. As you know, it is the right of any voter to propose an item for the warrant of that meeting, and to gather the signatures that will require the selectboard to put it before the gathered whole. Now, it's normal and proper that most of the work of town meeting is spent on local issues—the budget must be approved, after all. But it's by no means uncommon for larger issues to be raised from time to time.

"Many of you are old enough to remember, for example, the spring of 1982, when Ronald Reagan was president. That March, one hundred and ninety-two of Vermont's towns debated a resolution calling for a freeze in the testing and production of new nuclear weapons, and one hundred and sixty of them passed the measure. It carried no legal weight, of course—but it garnered immense publicity, and helped launch a global campaign. Before the year was out, a million protesters had gathered in Central Park, and twelve state legislatures, our own included, had endorsed the idea. By 1984, Reagan and Gorbachev were talking hard about a nuclear-free world, a goal we have yet to achieve but one we are much closer to than when that March evening began.

"But I want to tell you another story tonight, an older story. There can't be many left who went to a town meeting in

March of 1936, but those who did performed a great service for this state—in fact, Frank Bryan, Vermont's foremost political scientist, called what happened that night 'the most democratic expression of environmental consciousness in American history.' Some years prior, a New York engineer had proposed building a scenic highway along the backbone of our mountain range. For those of you who have traveled south, imagine a Green Mountain version of the Blue Ridge Parkway. It would, its boosters calculated, draw in millions each year in tourist dollars. And in the depths of the Depression it would provide work—work paid for with federal funds. Indeed the National Industrial Recovery Act would provide eighteen million dollars, and the State of Vermont would have had to pony up only five hundred thousand dollars. It was, its backers believed, a slam dunk, though of course at that point there was no such thing as a slam dunk. The Burlington papers supported it, the chamber of commerce supported it, every man of the right sort supported it. And the state legislature, which usually bows to men of the right sort, supported it too. In most states, that would have been the end of the story.

"But not in Vermont. The legislature asked for town meetings to vote on it the following spring. And it was in those town meetings that the real debate took place. Some did not like the idea of the federal government turning the center of the state into a national park. Many did not like the idea of that wild mountain spine turned into an auto playground. And even more did not like the idea that Vermont wasn't good enough already. One of the boosters of the plan, James P. Taylor, secretary of the Vermont Chamber of Commerce, made the mistake of saying what it was he most liked about the proposed road. By letting Vermonters ride to the heights, he said, it would cure them of their cussed and conservative 'valley-mindedness.'

"The votes were tallied slowly that day. Towns had other business, of course, and the parkway vote was often left for last. And we had no computers to instantly e-mail the votes, only town clerks and telephones. But when the last meeting had reported in, the sentiments of this state were clear. There was not enough money in Washington to buy the Green Mountains—the project had failed, 43,176 to 31,101. Bear and deer and moose and college coeds with rucksacks now wander where the gas stations and scenic pullouts would have been. And some of us are still narrow and conservative and cussed and valley-minded.

"If you're part of that fraternity, I hope you'll join the effort to make this town meeting special. Passing a resolution in support of a free Vermont will not make it happen, of course—no one knows yet quite how it would or could happen. But it would be a start—a signal to our legislature, and to the Congress in Washington, that we have begun to think small rather than large, that the time is approaching to hunker down instead of sprawl. At the very least it will give focus to our efforts, and allow us to see if we're just a small and loony minority, or if we're giving voice to a feeling that many people share but never really articulated, simply because the possibility never arose.

"Trance, I believe you have the high school girls' hockey scores from this evening?"

"Stowe six, Harwood four," she said. "Mount Mansfield three, Rice two; Rutland nil, Woodstock nil."

"Thanks for that. And thanks to you all for listening tonight. Remember that the Vermont Refugee Resettlement Program, which helps settle immigrants from around the world in our state, is holding volunteer orientations at their Colchester offices all month—call 655-1963. Perry, more Bob Marley as we sign off tonight?"

"No, we've been talking roads, so it has to be Motown? And it seemed to me Diana Ross said pretty much the same thing as the voters of Vermont. 'Stop! In the Name of Love,' number one with a bullet in the spring of 1965."

16

The rain was coming down in sheets outside the kitchen window, and Vern knew that Trance was calculating the same thing in her head as he was in his: How many feet of snow would this be, assuming it was falling as snow the way it should be in the very dead center of winter?

"Two feet anyway," he said, and sure enough she answered him without any hesitation.

"Two feet at least. Not that it would do me good—couldn't go for a ski if we had all the snow in the world. I hadn't figured out that being a fugitive would mean no exercise. I haven't worked out for four days—even when I was injured, I could go for a bike ride or something."

"Why'd you keep working out when you retired? Why didn't you go to pot like the rest of us ex-jocks?" he asked.

"Well, probably I will when I'm as old as you."

"No, but really?"

"Well, there was always a good reason of some kind. I was doing some coaching, and needed to be able to keep up with the kids."

"Trance, most of the best coaches I know have beer bellies you could balance a tray on."

"It's different for girls. But anyway, it's not the real reason. I've only ever had one thing I was really good at. The only time I ever felt really truly confident was with a gun on my back and skis on my feet."

"I remember that look you'd get," said Vern. "It was there almost from the beginning. It's why I was never great—I'd stand there, chest heaving, waiting to shoot, and I never really believed I was going to clean. But I can remember you coming into the range, looking fierce, never a doubt, like there was a wire between the gun and the target. When you did miss, you'd look surprised."

"But you found something else to do," said Trance. "I watched you last night in front of the microphone. There was no chance you were going to miss, and you knew it. You were even showing off a little. And with your job, you can do that your whole life. Athletes are done in their thirties if they're lucky, and that leaves a long time. So I keep training because I don't know what else I am. When I stop, I'll have to come up with an alternative."

"Maybe that's why you came and joined us here," said Vern.

"Maybe so," she said with a quick grin. "You taught me

biathlon, now you can teach me how to be a fugitive freedom fighter."

"Maybe so," he said. "Except the trouble is that I'm making it up as I go along."

They sat at the table, looking at the coffee, looking at the rain, looking at each other. "As long as I'm asking prying questions," said Vern, "let me ask one more. How come you never got married? Half the guys on the biathlon team were in love with you. In awe of you, but in love with you."

"Oh," she said, and paused briefly, staring down at her cup. "Because I like girls."

"Oh," he said, and paused briefly himself. "But still—this is Vermont. Girls have been getting married for years now. Half the babies in the state have two mommies."

"You're very open-minded for an old guy," she said.

"Well, it took a while. I spent a decade on the radio arguing against gay marriage for a whole lot of reasons. I mean, that's just how I grew up. But Fran, bless her, knew I just needed to know someone. And she knew her hairdresser. A stereotype, I know, but it was a small town. Anyway, we became friends, and then we became friends with his friend, and then with the kid they adopted, and pretty soon . . . Well, I guess I just thought about it and decided I had Fran, and everyone should be so lucky."

"I miss Fran," said Trance.

"I miss her too. But you've managed to avoid my question by getting me to talk about myself, which is a remarkably simple trick. So tell me, if you like girls, how come you're not with a girl?"

"Oh," said Trance. "Well, I guess because I'm not very good at it."

She saw Vern color a little, and giggled. "No, not that part. I'm a highly skilled athlete. That's what I'm good at. It's the talking part, the getting-to-know-people part. I don't have a very strong family background in that department, as you'll recall. My parents were good at . . . that part, which is why there are seven of us. But the rest was pretty brutal."

"I wish I had some good advice, but Fran pretty much handled the courting end of things in our relationship," said Vern. "I just followed her lead. But maybe you should talk to Sylvia."

"I hardly know her. Hard enough talking to you about this stuff, and I've known you all my life."

"Well, she's about the age to be your older sister. And . . . she likes girls too."

"How do you know *that?*" Trance asked quickly. "I mean, I thought she used to be married. Wasn't she just talking about her jerk of an ex-husband?"

"Maybe that's *why* she likes girls," he said. "Anyway, Perry and I were listening to her first class, and she told all the guys not to even try dating her, that she was a—that she liked girls."

"Huh," said Trance.

"Anyway, should I say something to Sylvia?"

"*No,*" said Trance. "Don't even think about it. *God,* no."

17

"I think we may need to do a little planning?" said Perry, emerging from his basement bedroom. "I'm getting the sense that they're searching pretty hard for us, and getting a little closer—some of those mirror sites are going down, and they're after the ISPs to give up all the data they've got."

"ISPs?" said Vern.

"Internet service providers. Eventually someone is going to figure out we're doing this over copper wire, and once that happens it's going to take them about ten minutes to follow that wire down this driveway."

"I think Perry's right," said Sylvia, who had the day's papers spread out before her. "For one thing, our neighbors know you're here."

"*What?*" said Vern.

"Remember the other day when you and Trance were out in the woods while we were doing firefighting practice?"

"I stayed way back—no one saw me."

"No one except Bucky and Jorene down the road. They're hunters. They have camera traps all through the woods—they sit there and watch critters, live on their computer. It's like the local version of the Discovery Channel. Anyway, you two had a nice long talk about seven feet from one. Jorene flagged me down on the way home today. She looked worried sick. She said she knew it was none of her business, and she liked you guys, but she was terrified I'd get in some kind of trouble."

"Are they going to turn us in?" Perry asked.

"No, of course not," said Sylvia. "They're *neighbors*. I mean, I cut a Christmas tree off their land every year. I helped their boy find a job. It's just that you're right. We're not going to stay invisible here forever.

"Anyway," she continued, "that's not the real trouble. You remember you said there'd be a reaction? I'd say it's starting."

She handed over the *Free Press*, with its lead headline: "Feds Join Barclay Hunt; Terror Ties Probed."

Montpelier—Gov. Leslie Bruce said today that more federal agents had joined Vermont State Police in the effort to track down radio host Vern Barclay, Olympic medalist Trance Harper, and other members of what he called "an anti-American conspiracy."

"At first we thought all this was kid stuff—an anti-Walmart publicity stunt," said Bruce. "But new evidence indicates that they are linked to Internet sites around the world, including some that also support terrorism. I've asked the FBI and the Federal

Communications Commission to help track down these fugitives before any of their stunts harm Vermonters."

Sources in the Boston FBI office said several agents from a private firm, Whitestream Security, had been dispatched to Vermont under government contract, along with sophisticated electronic equipment. "I want to assure the citizens of Vermont that they will be brought to justice quickly," said Bruce.

He added that residents circulating petitions in many communities to include Vermont secession on next month's town meeting warrants were "probably not criminals themselves, but just unwitting dupes."

"That's about what I'd expect," said Vern. "They're trying to scare people away, which will work pretty well. But frankly, this worries me more."

He was pointing to a full-page ad on page two of the paper, taken out by the state chapter of the AARP:

"DON'T RISK YOUR SOCIAL SECURITY," the headline read in 72-point type, and beneath it:

Many town meetings will next month consider a resolution for Vermont to secede from the United States. Remember that your monthly check comes from the FEDERAL government. Ask yourself how you'll survive without it!

A picture of Hap Hapson, president of the state's Farm Bureau, beamed from the facing page, above an article headlined: "Federal Payments Key to State's Agricultural Economy."

"Today's family farmer depends on the federal government for the assist to stay in business," Farm Bureau president Hap Hapson *said in a statement today. "If Vermont ever left the Union, there'd be no way for most of our members to keep farming."*

"You have to hand it to them," said Vern. "It took them a few days to get their act together, but I'd say they've started to do a decent job. Right now we're maybe terrorists, and definitely a threat to old folks and farmers. We know that's nonsense, but our real problem is we've got no way of answering back."

"We could do another podcast," said Perry.

"We could, and we will—but that's not going to do the trick here," said Vern. "The people who listen to those are the people who already support us, or at least lean in that direction. It's important to preach to the choir, but it's not enough. We need to reach lots of people, show them we're not scary. And we've got to do it before our story fades away—that's the real hope here. Time is always on the side of the status quo; we got people excited, but they know that excitement will fade away and people will just start thinking of the risk. If our momentum goes, we go with it."

"We kind of need television, don't we?" said Trance. "I mean, most of the people I grew up with watch television, not the Internet. They might read the newspaper, though not so much—what's on television is what's real."

"I hate to say it but you're right," said Vern. "I spent my life in radio, and over the long haul radio is more powerful—it's intimate, in your mind. But when something happens, people switch on the tube. Our problem is we don't have a TV station, and I don't think even Perry can give us one."

"Like I said, video is not really a possibility over copper," said Perry.

Vern sat back in his chair, holding his coffee cup in both hands, gazing at the drawn blinds. "I have a kind of idea," he said after a few minutes. "But it's going to mean us leaving here, and it's going to mean Sylvia going to jail."

"Then think of another idea," said Trance. "Because Sylvia is not going to jail."

"Oh, hon," said Sylvia with a smile. "I've known I was going to jail since the day Vern arrived. Let's at least hear it out."

"Also, we may have to burn down your house."

"In for a dime . . . anyway, my ex-husband built it, and it's about as dark as he was."

"Well," he said. "As you can tell, it's probably not a great plan. But you know Horace LaRossette, right?"

"Of course. He's been doing the nightly newscast for my whole life," said Sylvia.

"Longer than that," said Vern. "Sometimes I think he was there when Philo Farnsworth turned the first TV dial. I've known him most of my life, and I'm counting on two things. He literally can't resist a scoop, and he's in the back pocket of the governor."

18

A shiny new black Jeep Cherokee with temporary dealer's tags cruised to a stop outside the WVTV studios, and a man in dark glasses and a heavy beard reached across to open the passenger door. "Climb in, Mr. LaRossette," he said. "You can put that camera equipment on the backseat."

"Where are we going?" said the anchor, who was wearing a navy suit with a yellow tie.

"Well, *I'm* going back to Racine Jeep Eagle around the corner, so I can finish my test drive," said the man. "And after that I don't know where you're going, but I do know that you're supposed to wear these," he added, handing him a pair of wraparound dark glasses like the ones that old folks wear after cataract surgery. When he put them on, LaRossette found they'd been duct-taped from the inside to shut out all light. He started to protest, but even as he began, the car slowed to a halt, and his door opened. A woman's hand slipped inside his and led him to the front seat of another car; he could hear his camera bag being switched from one backseat to the other.

"Hello," said the woman, once she'd strapped him into his seat belt. "This won't take long—less than an hour."

"These glasses are ridiculous! I've never been treated like this in forty-two years of journalism!" said LaRossette.

"I'm so sorry," she said soothingly. "And what a nice suit you're wearing!"

"Do you think so? It's cashmere," he said.

"Really!" she said. "And where did you get it?"

"It's provided courtesy of Men's Wearhouse, at the University Mall," he said. "I go out every three months and pick out five new ones."

"That sounds like fun."

"Oh, you have no idea. It's the best part of the job. The news is the same every day, but the suits change constantly. And people pay attention! Sometimes I get e-mail when I wear a new suit. People send ties!"

The drive proceeded smoothly, as Horace discussed the number of regional Emmy awards he had won (twenty-two), the number of national Edward R. Murrow awards (six), the number of minor celebrities he knew on a first-name basis (almost infinite), how it was he was able to look so young after so many years of working so hard ("good genes," though Sylvia thought she saw the small line from a tuck job under his left ear), why younger people were ruining the TV business (had not worked their way up, no sense of history), and some funny things that Walter Cronkite (Walt) had told him once at a convention. "He gave me the best advice of my career, too. He said, 'Horace, if you're going to make people like you, you have to pretend to like them.' So that's exactly what I do, with everyone I meet. And I find he was absolutely right."

"I guess he was, because I sure do like you, Mr. LaRossette," said Sylvia. "And so I'm very sad to say that we're at the end of our ride. You'll be inside in just a few minutes, and then you'll be able to take off those silly glasses." She glided to a halt, and Perry opened the door, reached in, and took the newsman's elbow.

"This way, sir, right this way," he said. "My friends will get your gear."

A moment later he was sitting in the kitchen of Sylvia's house, where the shades had been drawn and the cupboards stripped—it looked like a kitchen in a showroom. "Sorry about those glasses, Horace—you can take them off now," said Vern, and when the anchor did, blinking in the light, he saw three people sitting in front of him on kitchen chairs, with only a Free Vermont flag as a backdrop.

"I think you know Trance Harper," said Vern.

"Of course I do—I have the picture of the two of us with the Olympic medal hanging on my wall," said LaRossette.

"And this is our friend Perry Alterson," said Vern. "He's another of you big-city Burlington boys."

"Vern—I hope you don't think I'm going to ask you

puffball questions just because we've known each other forever," said LaRossette. "I've got a list right here in my pocket,
and just as soon as I get this camera working . . ." He was
fussing with the tripod and the microphone connection.
"They showed me how to do this at the station today. I wish
you'd let me bring along a cameraman."

"Maybe I could help you with that," said Perry after watching for a few minutes. He quickly connected the cords, set up
the battery pack, even took the lens cap off the front. "I think
you just need to press this button when you want to talk, sir,"
he said.

"Yes, that's exactly right," said LaRossette. "You'd think
you'd been in the business as long as I have, you know the
equipment almost as well as I do. Well, let's get started.

"First question—and I warned you, these aren't going to
be easy. The Farm Bureau says that you'd put Vermont farmers out of business. How do you respond?"

Vern looked at Perry. "Horace, I'm an old farmboy, so I
could give you my opinion. But let's hear some facts and fig-
ures first—and Perry is our data specialist."

"Well," said Perry, nervously, "in 1947, there were 11,206
dairy farms in Vermont; 1957, 9,512; 1967, 4,729. In 1977,
there were 3,531; in 1987, 2,771; in 1997, 1,908; 2008, 1,273;
and in 2012, there were 1,075. Last year the number was down
to 862."

"What that means, if you ask me, is simple," said Vern.
"The Farm Bureau and the federal government have already

done a fine job of putting Vermont farmers out of business. And it's pretty obvious why they've been so successful, isn't it? The USDA has spent the last six decades trying to make farms bigger and bigger. The subsidies go to the big guys, the ag schools spend their time working on how to make farms bigger. They've taken the most fertile continent on the earth and turned it into a corn-syrup factory. The dairies we still have left in Vermont seem enormous to me—a thousand cows! But even they are tiny compared to the ones in California or Minnesota or Arizona. Those guys have ten thousand cows, and so they set the price of milk. Which is so low that even our big dairies can't make any money. They have to hire undocumented migrants because they're the only ones who will work for wages that low—without them, no milk. You've seen them living half hidden all over the Champlain Valley, Horace. Anyway, the get-big-or-get-out farm stuff from the feds was just the usual foolishness that mostly hurt small farmers—except that now, as the climate goes kaflooey, it's going to come back and bite all of us. Because we don't grow much actual food here in Vermont anymore—about five percent of what we eat. Twenty times as much milk as we drink, but only a twentieth of the food we eat. We want farmers growing food that people want to eat—we want slaughterhouses in Vermont again, and canneries, and grain mills. Not big food so we can get salmonella from some feedlot in Indiana, but small food, so we can get dinner from our neighbors. So we have some security."

"Let's talk about security, then," said Horace. "A lot of us are depending on Social Security to ease us through our Golden Years. But if we left the country, those checks would stop coming. Aren't you set on starving out Grandma and Grandpa?"

"Well, the first thing to say is, if you're depending on Social Security, you may want to think again," said Vern. "At the moment its promised benefits exceed its projected income by trillions . . ."

19

Six hours later Trance, Perry, and Vern were together again, but this time in a small motel room on the outskirts of Barre. A friend of Sylvia's had rented the room, and lingered in the gathering dusk to hand them the key.

"Don't bother unpacking," said Vern. "We're only here a couple of hours. All we need is the computer."

Perry was already unpacking his MacBook Pro. "Thank God we're back in the modern world," he said. "That copper connection was—look, here we go. We can see everything the camera sees. Hooray for night-vision."

"That's the same game camera Syl's neighbors were watching us on?" asked Trance.

"Yep," said Vern. "We rotated it a few degrees, so we could get a basic view of the front of Syl's house. It's not perfect, but it will let us know once they've arrived. Which shouldn't be long. Assuming Horace read the business card he picked up so inelegantly, and assuming he called the governor on the way home, and assuming Tommy Augustus never asked himself why desperate terrorists left a business card with their host's address on the floor, assuming all those things, the state police should be arriving any minute."

"Do you think this motel has a gym?" asked Trance.

"I doubt it, but you can't use it anyway," said Vern. "But I'll count push-ups for you if you want."

"I've been doing push-ups and sit-ups for the last week. I need to *move*," said Trance.

"Not right now though," said Perry. "Something's happening."

The action through the game camera was a little jerky, and hard to make out, but it looked as if six or eight large vehicles with flashing lights had pulled into the dirt driveway in front of Sylvia's house. Men were piling out, rifles in hand, and taking position behind the vehicles. One man, ducked down behind an SUV, was talking into a microphone while another held the bullhorn over the roof.

"I wish these cameras came with audio," said Perry.

"Normally deer don't talk much," said Trance.

"Doesn't matter. That's Tommy Augustus and he's saying something original like 'Come out with your hands up.' Which means, Perry, that it's time for the firecrackers."

Perry hit a button, and though they couldn't hear anything, they hoped that six loud pops had sounded from an upstairs corner window of Syl's house. It took about five seconds before they knew the device had worked—that was the moment when every gun in the driveway seemed to let loose at once, with a fusillade that lit up the evening. In the sudden flash they could see another vehicle coming up the driveway.

"Oh good," said Vern. "Turn on WVTV."

"*. . . LaRossette reporting live from the Channel 3 Mobile CrimeCatcher Tank here in Starksboro. We're exclusively outside the home of Sylvia Granger, where Vern Barclay, Trance Harper, and their associates are holed up, according to state police.*"

Horace was crouched behind the truck, and now they could hear the gunfire loud and clear. "I wish he'd stop blocking the house with the truck," said Vern. "But judging from the glow over his shoulder, I'd suspect the kerosene has worked and that house is 'fully involved,' as we used to say at the firehouse."

". . . Chief Augustus," Horace was yelling. "Can you join us here?"

Tommy Augustus crawled from his vehicle over to the newstank, removing his hat long enough to make sure his hair was combed down underneath.

"Chief Augustus, what's happening in there?" LaRossette yelled.

"Horace, we managed to track down the terrorists to this location. We came under fire, and then we returned fire. This is the end of the line for terror in Vermont."

"The noise is deafening," said Horace.

"We're using lots of new equipment that the feds have loaned us for this operation," said Augustus, with a grin. "The rocket-propelled grenades are making most of that noise. Those are desperate people in there and I'm not taking any chances with the lives of my men. We are setting an example here."

At that moment a new sound began to grow on the TV—the wail of a siren approaching fast. The WVTV camera swung around, and in the orange light of the burning house it was easy to see a familiar fire truck, with Sylvia at the wheel in full fire gear. It ground to a halt next to the vehicles, and men jumped from the cab and began unrolling hose.

"Stop!" screamed Augustus. "Get down."

"Who are you?" said Sylvia.

"Chief Augustus of the Vermont State Police," he said. "Who are you?"

"Chief Granger of the Starksboro Volunteer Fire Department," said Sylvia. "And this is my house you're shooting at."

"We're only shooting at it because your terrorists have been shooting at us," said Tommy.

"What are you talking about, terrorists?" said Sylvia. "I've lived in that house for twenty years and I've never once seen a terrorist."

"Are you telling me that Trance Harper and Vern Barclay and that kid aren't in that house?" said Tommy.

"I was there three hours ago, before I went down to the firehouse for our monthly meeting, and there wasn't a soul there but me," said Sylvia.

"That's ridiculous," said Tommy. "They were shooting at us."

"Was anyone hit?" she asked. "Do I need to call in the ambulance crew?"

"Not for us," said Tommy. "They missed."

"Wait," said Sylvia. "Weren't you on TV last week saying that Trance Harper was extremely dangerous, a trained sniper who could kill from a mile away? How'd she miss you?"

Augustus looked a little panicked in the camera lights. He hesitated for a moment.

"You tell them, Horace. This is the hideout, right?"

"Hey, you weren't supposed to tell that I—"

"This is the hideout where the gang brought you this morning, right?"

"Well, remember, I never actually saw the outside. I was hooded," said LaRossette. "But I can easily identify the kitchen," he added.

"You better do it pretty quick," said Sylvia, looking straight into the camera. "Because it looks to me like the kitchen isn't going to be there much longer. And if you really think there are people inside, maybe you should let my crew put this fire out," she added.

"No!" said Tommy. "Those people are armed and dangerous. And you—you're, you're under arrest for harboring fugitives from the law."

He pulled a pair of handcuffs from his belt and clamped her wrists behind her back. Sylvia looked at the camera and said,

"I'm starting to see why these people want a free Vermont—I mean, I'm being arrested for trying to put out a fire in my own house. Mr. LaRossette, it's very nice to meet you in person. You look shorter than on TV, but that's an awfully nice suit you have on underneath that Kevlar vest."

"Wardrobe provided courtesy of Men's Wearhouse at University Mall," he said, as Augustus led Sylvia away into the night. "We're here exclusively at the site of what state police are calling a terrorist hideout in Starksboro." A wide shot from the cameraman holding his lens above the roof of a police car filled the screen, showing the house already caving in, with a column of fire rising high into the night.

20

Sylvia, looking radiant as her blond hair spilled over an orange prison jumpsuit, walked down the steps of the Washington County courthouse the next morning on the arms of two men in suits, and flanked by fourteen others—eleven men and three women. They stopped at a makeshift lectern in front of dozens of reporters, and one of the men stepped to the microphone.

"Good morning," he said. "My name is David Fenton, and I will be serving as media coordinator for the team representing Ms. Granger in the days ahead. She will answer questions in a moment, but first let me bring you up to date on the day's proceedings.

"Ms. Granger was released this morning after an appearance before Judge Lem Harkness in Superior Court. The State of Vermont asked for bail of ten million dollars, arguing that she was a flight risk. Our team argued that she was a long-term resident of the community, residing in the same house for twenty years until the State of Vermont burned it to the ground last evening. We further informed the judge that we know of no physical or other evidence to substantiate the charge that she harbored terrorists, and moved to have all charges dismissed, a motion the judge took under advisement. In addition, we filed suit this morning in state court seeking fifty million dollars in damages for the destruction of her home and the mental distress caused by forcing her to watch, handcuffed, as that home burned to the ground. Now, if there are some questions?"

The reporters started shouting, and Fenton pointed at a tall man in the first row.

"Anne Galloway, VTDigger.org," she said. "Can you describe the scene at your home last night?"

"Not very well," she said. "When I was led away, my home was fully involved—the fire had spread to every part of the structure. It's what we call a Class V structure, ordinary wood construction. My fire department was on hand and the tank of the pumper was full; not only that but there's a pond by the house that would have let us spray for an hour. But law enforcement prevented us from fighting the fire, which is probably just as well since as far as I could see they were busy, for reasons unclear to me, keeping a heavy gunfire on the premises. It was pretty interesting, and if it hadn't been my own house, it might have been kind of fun to watch—I am told much of Vermont viewed it live on television. But I was led away before it was over; my assistant chief informed me earlier this morning that there was nothing left but a few smoldering timbers with a lot of state and federal investigators sifting through them. They wouldn't let him anywhere near."

"Paul Heintz, *Bennington Banner*. Was there anyone else in your house last night?"

"I was divorced eight years ago and live alone," said Sylvia. "My dog died last summer. Thank God I waited to get a new puppy."

"Tim Timmins, WVTV. But the state police insist that Vern Barclay and Trance Harper died in your house last night. In fact, tonight at seven we're broadcasting their unseen last interviews, in a special series, 'Voices from Beyond the Grave.' Are you saying you didn't even know them?"

Sylvia paused, and looked at the man on her left, who gave a slight nod.

"Well," she said, choosing her words carefully. "Everyone knows Vern Barclay. I mean, I drank my coffee listening to him since I was in high school. And he interviewed me when I started my school, the School for New Vermonters. Trance Harper—I'm not a big sports fan. But I was watching when she raised that flag over the new arena, and what she said about big and small was the smartest thing I'd heard in a very long time. I doubt if my television works very well anymore, but I'll make sure to watch those interviews tonight—and I'll sure hope that they're still alive somewhere, because it seems to me we need them in this state. I mean, I thought that before, but after last night I really think it. I may not have a house in Starksboro right at the moment, but I imagine they'll still let me come to town meeting, and I'm going to vote for a free Vermont."

"Angelo Lynn, *Addison Independent*. Ms. Granger, I've been a reporter here in Vermont for a very long time, and I've never seen anyone with sixteen lawyers. How can you afford this much legal . . . firepower?"

"Um, that's a very good question," said Sylvia.

"I'll take that one," said Fenton, stepping to the microphone. "Only fourteen of us are attorneys. I'm a media relations specialist, as is Mr. Erskine Hunnewell, former vice president of the global PR firm, Hill and Knowlton. Our entire team is working pro bono, because we had the pleasure of studying at Ms. Granger's school when we retired to Vermont. She taught us a variety of skills, which we now pursue—when I got the call this morning about this court appearance, I was preparing to cut firewood on my property. While wearing, I might add, chaps and hearing protection," he said, glancing at Sylvia, who beamed back.

"But even though we are retired, we retain some of our old skills. Ms. Granger's representation includes the former general counsels of Pillsbury, Xerox, and International Harvester"—at the mention of each company one of the men nodded slightly—"as well as the former attorney general of New Jersey, the former deans of the law schools at Harvard and Princeton, and judges from the Fourth and Sixth federal circuit courts. In fact, our team is slightly larger than this group—two of us, including the lead counsel for the Senate committee that investigated the Waco shootings, are on hand at the site of Ms. Granger's former home, watchdogging the forensic investigation. We believe she will have . . . *adequate* representation," he concluded, unable to suppress a grin.

"We will be holding daily press briefings, but for now we need to get Ms. Granger some rest. Thank you very much," he said, and he led Sylvia into a Subaru Forester with tinted windows that was waiting at the curb. As it drove away, with reporters chasing it down the road shouting questions, every camera caught the "Barclay for Prime Minister" bumper sticker on the back.

21

"*Tonight, a WVTV exclusive report. Those of you who were watching our live coverage last night from the Channel 3 Crime-Catcher Tank know that a Starksboro farmhouse burned to the ground. FBI experts continue to search the site, looking for evidence to back up the claim from Montpelier that it's the grave of longtime radio host Vern Barclay and Olympic heroine Trance Harper.*"

"I would have liked to be a fly on the wall when Tommy Augustus met the governor today," said Vern. "Leslie Bruce may not be the absolute sharpest chisel in the tool drawer, but he's a good enough politician not to want to watch live as his chief of police handcuffs the chief of a local fire department to keep her from saving her own home."

"*. . . What you don't know is that I, Horace LaRossette, was in that farmhouse earlier in the day. Or in some other farmhouse, maybe—I was wearing a blindfold. Anyway, I was able to conduct* *an in-depth interview with Harper, Barclay, and a third young man, Percy Alterman."*

"Well, that's pretty close to Perry Alterson," said Perry. "And after I fixed his camera."

"If the authorities are correct, these are their last words. They are literally speaking . . . from Beyond the Grave. I asked them a series of hard-hitting questions about their hopes for Vermont, and the conduct of their underground campaign. Now, in their own words, these fellow Vermonters."

The picture shifted to videotape from Sylvia's kitchen, though there was no clue beyond the blue wall behind the three as they answered questions.

". . . Farm Bureau says that you'd put Vermont farmers out of business. How do you respond?"

"Horace, I'm an old farmboy, so I could give you my opinion. But let's hear some facts and . . ."

Vern had never gotten used to seeing himself on TV. He was comfortable with his voice, maybe a little proud even ("not silver, but a bit of pewter," was how he thought of it) but he found it distracting to watch himself, even in the best of times. *And this is not the best of times,* he found himself thinking. *I look old, I look tired. Do I look a little crazy?* He closed his eyes.

". . . the first thing to say is, If you're depending on Social Security you may want to think again," he was telling Horace. Eyes closed, it sounded okay. *"At the moment its promised benefits exceed its projected income by trillions of dollars—that's trillions with a T. In any event, it shouldn't vanish simply because we leave*

the Union; Americans who move abroad continue to receive their checks, because it's just the return on the money they've invested throughout their lives. If Vermont became 'abroad,' our seniors should be protected."

"Well, you may not be treasonous," said Horace, "but the Bruce administration has made some serious charges that need addressing. Most of all—why are you engaging in terrorism?"

"Whoa, Horace," said Vern, "I think that's what the lawyers call 'a leading question.' So far as I can tell, we haven't fired a shot or blown up a bomb or threatened to do anything of the kind. It's true that Perry and I did manage to, um, fill the new Walmart with a different kind of crap than the crap they sell, but in terms of volume it was considerably less manure than one of our big corporate mega-dairies produces in a single day, and none of it washed straight down into the lake. Except for that, we've done nothing but talk."

"But what about you, Trance?" asked LaRossette. "The government says you're a highly trained markswoman."

"Mr. LaRossette, I've been shooting things since I was a little girl. I shot coyotes on the farm, I shot targets when I was an athlete. And I went to Iraq and shot people—five of them. Five shots and five kills and I'm not ashamed—I did what my country asked. But I'm not ever doing it again, not for anything. I'm done shooting people. And even if I wasn't, I'm a good enough soldier to know that you don't choose your opponent's weapons—the government has more guns than we could ever hope for, and I imagine they're just looking for an excuse to use them. This is an entirely nonviolent campaign, at least on our side."

"Well, *okay*," said LaRossette, who seemed a little startled by her sternness. "*And may I just say thanks for the people of Vermont for your service to your country. At WVTV we honor all our warriors.*"

Trance just looked at him, a look that lasted long seconds till the coverage cut back to the studio, and to LaRossette, who still looked a little startled. "*That was yesterday. Today Trance Harper may be dead. She claims she'd laid down her weapons; the government insists they were fired on from inside that farmhouse. Those may have been her last words—we'll keep following this story.*"

"*In Enosburg Falls tonight, a two-car accident has left a Chittenden County man with a broken leg. That story and your warm weekend weather still ahead here on Channel 3.*"

22

Trance and Perry were sprawled across the two twin beds in the motel room, boots up on the dingy bedspreads. Vern sat in a wobbly chair by the tiny desk, idly playing with the drinking glass, "sanitarily wrapped for your protection." The place stank of stale smoke, and he thought of how strange the smell seemed now. For most of his life, it had meant "restaurant" or "bar" or "airplane," and he hadn't hardly ever even noticed. But two decades of no smoking laws meant it was now exotic, and linked tight to poverty. Only the lowest end of clubs or motels still let anyone light up. It actually smelled okay, he thought.

"So what do we do now?" he asked, and then proceeded to provide an answer, since that seemed to have become his role. "I guess we better get back up on the air and put out some more podcasts—see if we can build our momentum back up. Do we have what we need?" he asked Perry.

"Well, I took the most important equipment from Sylvia's house," Perry said. "I've got the modem, and the microphone, and my laptop. If we've got a phone line, we can probably do it, though it won't be simple going through a motel switchboard. But"—and here he paused for a long minute—"I'm not sure it's such a good idea?"

"Why not?" said Vern. "We can find another phone line."

"No, not that," said Perry. "It's—the timing seems wrong. I mean, right now they're going around telling everyone we're dead. That means we're ghosts, kind of? So if we jump out and go 'boo,' everyone will notice. But—the longer we wait maybe the more they'll notice?"

"I see the point," said Trance. "We're not dead, which is nice. But we're kind of dead, which is nice in a way too. If we lie low for a little while, people will have to figure out what to do on their own a little—it's like when you were coaching us. At a certain point you'd say, 'You know your own bodies now, you know what they need.' It made us feel more . . . independent. Which is kind of the idea?"

"Anyway," said Perry. "Don't you think those lawyers helping Sylvia are going to keep things going for a little while? Won't they kind of 'keep the story alive,' like you're always saying? And that way we can plan a real return? Something that will wow people more than another podcast?"

Vern thought for a moment, unwrapping the drinking glass from its hygienic jacket and then wrapping it back up. He'd gotten used to being in charge, he thought—he'd just made them all burn down Sylvia's house. But as he thought a little harder, he realized the only real argument for his plan was that it would let him talk sooner, and he liked to talk. After a lifetime at the radio, talk was his default setting; if he wasn't talking, then it felt like events were just passing him by. But of course, he reminded himself, that's how most people felt most of the time, and anyway even if you did have a microphone and a signal, it usually was just chatter anyway. "You're right," he said. "If we wait, we can maybe make it count for more. Good call.

"But," he added, "we're going to need a new base of operations. We've got ten days to go till town meeting—after that Perry and I are going to have to turn ourselves in, I imagine. But we want to keep this running for as long as we can, so we need someplace they're not going to find us. I have an idea— you might think it's a little creepy, but I'm pretty sure it's safe."

Five hours later, shortly after midnight, Trance steered the old Saab up to a loading dock at the back of a building with a single security light. A door opened at the top of the ramp, and the three piled out of the car, grabbing their few bags and walking quickly up and into an industrial kitchen, where they were greeted by a very old woman wearing slippers and a down jacket with the U.S. Olympic logo.

"Hi, Trance," the woman said, giving her a hug. "Glad to see you. And you must be Perry," she said, moving in for another embrace. "I like your hair. I think I'm going to do that. Is it true you never have to wash it?

"Hello, son," the woman added, turning to Vern. "I was worried you were dead there for a few minutes till I saw that Sylvia woman. She was practically winking at Horace, that dummy. You remember I had him in second grade. And Tommy Augustus—a policeman?"

"Hi, Mother," said Vern, a little sheepishly. "I missed you."

"Well, we've all been listening to your tape recordings," she said. "I put them on my Facebook page. Except no more pussyfooting around with Social Security—just say that Vermont is going to pay it instead. We don't care who pays it as long as it comes. We're old and we vote!" she added. "Anyway, come with me to your new hideout."

She led the way through the deserted kitchen, and into a service elevator, and onto a third-floor hall, dark except for lights above each door. "This is the Memory Care wing," she said. "Which means that no one here remembers anything. And this is Martha Oxbow's room. Perry, Martha's my age, and she was practically a second mom to Vern growing up. And practically a second grandmother to Trance." They entered the door without knocking and closed it behind them. An old woman lay under a blanket on one bed, breathing evenly. She appeared to be awake, and turned to look at them, but her stare was blank.

"Good evening, dear," said Mrs. Barclay, taking her hands. "I've brought Vern and Trance and their friend Perry to stay with you. That kind of hair is just the fashion now."

She turned to the others. "The other bed is empty because

her roommate checked out yesterday, if you know what I mean. And I've told the director to leave it empty for a while—she knows something's up, obviously, but ever since I organized the march on the capitol for more Medicare reimbursement last winter, she's pretty much gone along with whatever I want."

She kept stroking her friend's hands, which were almost rigid. "Those two extra cots are for family to sleep with their loved ones. Martha has a private nurse, but they gave her a week off; there's no family left to visit, which is one reason I thought this would be good for her. She spent half her life listening to your voice, son—it will make her calm. And they say that any kind of activity is good; just remember that somewhere in there she can hear you. I'll be bringing you your food. And Perry—Vern says you need a phone line—there's a jack right there next to the bed. No switchboard. But shouldn't I just plug you into the home's Ethernet? We've got monster bandwidth."

23

At eight the next morning the door to the room burst open, and a rolling cart came clattering in, pushed by an unseen force that turned out to be Mrs. Barclay, barely tall enough to see over the stack of trays.

"Breakfast this morning is Cream of Wheat, which is very popular with the management because it's difficult to choke on," she said. "Of course, it's also difficult to eat, so I also got you a box of Dunkin' Donuts. I know we don't like Starbucks, but Dunkin' Donuts is okay, don't you think? They advertised on your program for years, and they bring the orphans to Fenway Park every game. Anyway, their coffee is much better than Starbucks, not that I've had Starbucks except on rest stops on I-89 where you don't really have much choice do you? I have honey-dipped, and for Trance chocolate honey-dipped. Perry, I didn't know what you liked."

They'd all been sleeping when this small explosion of

smell and talk went off, and by the time they were fully awake, Mrs. Barclay was already up on the bed spoon-feeding hot cereal to her old friend. "What do you think, Martha? Exciting in here for once. Nice to have a roommate that isn't about to croak, though these guys could be hauled off to jail at any moment, I suppose. Trance, see, this is easy—she can't hold the spoon, but she'll suck the food right off it."

"I can do that," said Perry. "I used to feed my grandmother." He climbed up on the bed, with a cruller in one hand, and took the spoon from Vern's mother.

"Now you've got a handsome young man bringing you breakfast in bed, Martha," said Mrs. Barclay. "And he's got more hair than you and I combined."

"Doughnuts," groaned Trance, grabbing one. "Mama Barclay, I haven't had any exercise in weeks, not since I started hanging out with these fugitives. I can't tell you how stir-crazy I'm going. And how fat I'm getting."

"Not very fat," said Mrs. Barclay. "I mean, I'm an expert. You actually look better than you have for years, dear. Doesn't she, Martha? But you can use the water aerobics pool tonight if you want—Aquacise ends at six and we'll figure out a way to sneak you down. You wear a float and you jog in the water—it looks stupid, but Annie Nichols next door to me does it. Of course she'd need to because she has serious cocktails every night. She makes them for the men in the model train club, but they hardly pay her any attention, they're too busy talking about narrow-gauge this, and Lionel that. Still, they are men, which is something. And speaking of men, you might want to watch the news this morning. Your friend Sylvia and her harem of lawyers will be holding their press conference at ten, which means it should be done in time for your programs, Martha. Martha likes the interview programs with the bad people. I can remember her telling me, 'I may not have done anything very special with my life, but at least my children didn't grow up to be Prostitutes and Proud of It.' Also she likes that man who screams at you about stocks at night, and honks the horn. He reminds us of the men who stood outside the naked lady tent at the Tunbridge Fair when we were girls. We didn't want to see the naked ladies—we could just look at ourselves—but we liked listening to him talk." As she talked, she was gathering up the plates and napkins and cups, and pushing her cart out the door. "Goodbye, children, take good care of Martha," she said as she disappeared.

"Your mother is amazing," said Perry, wiping the corners of Martha Oxbow's mouth with a damp napkin.

"It's never been much secret where you learned to talk, Vern," said Trance, who was doing sit-ups.

"Maybe we should turn on the TV," said Vern, who found himself feeling a little weary.

David Fenton was standing once more on the steps of the county courthouse, which Trance and Vern knew was about five hundred yards from where they reclined, watching with

Perry and Martha. Fenton had his arm protectively on Sylvia's shoulder as he read a statement from a sheet of paper.

"We are pleased to announce this morning that after negotiations, Governor Bruce has agreed to settle one phase of our lawsuit in connection with the burning of Ms. Granger's home. The State of Vermont will pay for the construction of a new home on the site, with work to begin immediately. Happily, Ms. Granger's former students include two of America's most renowned architects, A. Archer McClune, the founding partner of McClune McCloskey, and Nathaniel Gunderson, who was responsible for the award-winning art museums in Fort Worth, Oakland, and Montevideo. Out of respect for their new state, they will offer their services pro bono, and indeed have already completed one set of preliminary drawings that includes a fifty-seat theater for Ms. Granger to conduct her classes.

"This settlement in no way prejudices Ms. Granger's action against the state for mental distress caused by being forced to watch the destruction of her home. However, we have dropped our award demand to forty million dollars from fifty million, given the estimated cost of the new structure. And we're happy to report that the cost of her new home will be borne not by taxpayers but by the state's insurers, who are continuing their own investigation of last week's unfortunate events.

"We have time for a few questions—Mr. Totten?" he said.

"Shay Totten, *Seven Days*. Do you guys think that this quick settlement has anything to do with the polls that show eighty-seven percent of Vermonters outraged by the state's handling of the fire scene?"

"We're not able to speculate as to motive," said Fenton. "But," he added with a small smile, "we were impressed by the spirit of *urgency* the governor's attorneys brought to the table. It would be nice if all negotiations could be completed in such timely fashion."

"Dick Drysdale, *Randolph Herald*. Have your forensic experts uncovered any evidence that Vern Barclay or the others were in the house that night?"

"Our investigators have not been granted full access to the scene by the FBI or the state police, but we understand that to date, those authorities have not recovered any shell casings or other ballistic evidence from sources other than their own weaponry. However, those questions might better be directed to Chief Augustus."

"Follow-up, if I may. Chief Augustus said last night that the fact that no one's heard from Barclay or the rest is proof they died in the fire."

"Perhaps Chief Augustus should read Mr. Conan Doyle's account of the dog that failed to bark in the night," said Fenton. "Or, as my ethics professor used to say, 'Absence of proof is not proof of absence.' He was, I think, quoting the English poet William Cowper, and if so, that same man also remarked, 'A fool must now and then be right, by chance.' So I guess we will have to wait and see what turns up. As Cowper himself further remarked, 'God moves in mysterious ways.'"

"Mark Johnson, WDEV," said a man in a sports jacket with a furrowed brow. "A question for Ms. Granger—I know you said that the fugitives weren't in your house that evening, at least as far as you knew. I'm just wondering whether—if they are still alive—you'd like to meet them in the future?"

Sylvia smiled. "Let me answer this way. The layout of my new house includes a full radio studio and an extensive home gym. Any time Vern Barclay and Trance Harper want to use my home as a base, it will be theirs. When the governor burned down my house, he turned me into a Vermont patriot—there will be a large flagpole at the head of the driveway, and it will fly the Free Vermont flag twenty-four hours a day."

As they watched Sylvia disappear once more into the Subaru with the tinted windows, her phalanx of lawyers closing ranks behind her, they were all grinning. "I was a little worried about burning down her house—guess I needn't have been," said Vern. "And if the governor is building her a mansion, I imagine it means he's well and truly scared. People may fret about Social Security and farm aid and all the rest, but it's hard to focus on arguments like that when they're watching the state police keep a fire chief from putting out a fire in her own home."

"It's not just here," said Perry, who had his laptop out. "It's the YouTube of the week. Three million views. There are comments from every state."

"Which means we need to close the sale," said Vern. "Town meeting is about a week away, and it's almost the moment for us to come back from the dead. And this time not just a podcast. Perry, we've got to figure out a way to do real radio. Live radio."

24

Vern was sitting in the same straight-backed chair where he'd spent most of the past two days. He'd talked with his mother, with Trance, with Perry, taken a turn feeding Martha Oxbow, watched Jim Cramer holler about natural gas as a counter-cyclical play, but mostly he'd thought.

First, about the broadcast. He had no doubt people would be listening—ever since he'd called Mark Johnson and told him that he wanted to take over his show for a half hour, the state's media had talked of little else. He hadn't spoken with Mark for more than forty seconds when he'd called to set up the broadcast, afraid that the police might be able to track his phone call, but they'd known each other for decades and Johnson was vouching that it was really him. "I listened to his voice every morning for decades," he'd said. "If it wasn't him, it was the best impressionist in Vermont."

So Vern knew people would listen—he just wasn't certain

what he'd say. He'd gotten into this almost by accident; if Perry hadn't flooded the Walmart, his broadcast from the store would have been a nice way of saying goodbye to radio but not much more. Instead, now, people were pasting bumper stickers on their Subarus nominating him for prime minister of a new country. He knew he wasn't going to run anything—the question was, did it really make sense for there to be something new for *anyone* to run?

I mean, he thought, the U.S. has *worked*, not perfectly but perfectly well, for a very long time—as long as I've been around, and before that. Trump, true. But we survived Nixon. And Warren Harding. What kind of stunt was it to insist that he'd figured out some better future? He'd spent his life talking on the radio, which meant he "knew" about current affairs—but he'd never gotten his hands dirty in Montpelier, never made a budget, never run a hearing, never had a lobbyist come down hard on him. *Am I just being a romantic? Am I just leading people on?* He'd already burned down Sylvia's house, though thank God that seemed to be turning out okay. But Trance's life had been turned upside down, and now his mother was involved, and that was just the beginning—he was asking tens of thousands of people to do something a little dangerous and more than a little weird. What if they started down this path and their Social Security *did* get cut off?

The worry was more acute because, now that he had broadband, Perry would show him some new nugget of news every few hours. The idea of breaking away had begun to really spread. In California, polls were showing a quarter of the state wanting out of the Union—and they were the planet's fifth-largest economy, not some San Marino or Liechtenstein. In the cities sprinkled across the nation's red interior, people were researching Siena and Florence: why not city-states again, some were asking—after all, most of the country's wealth, most of its great institutions, most of its "creative class," most of its brewpubs were housed in the enclaves that blinked blue against the red sea on election night. Serious legal scholars were publishing treatises on *Texas v. White*, the 1869 Supreme Court case that held secession illegal; how was that really possible, they asked, in a nation that had begun its life by seceding from the British Empire? Four of the NBA's biggest stars had held a press conference the night before, saying that they wanted to see its name shortened to the Basketball Association because they were none too happy with the nation just now; in south Texas, Hispanic leaders were holding an informal referendum for their constituents: "Which Side of the Wall Do We Want to Be On?"

Such talk worried Vern as much as it cheered him. Yes, this time around it was the good-hearted folks who were talking about seceding, not the slaveholders. Still, it was a large step, and one he'd stumbled into more or less by accident. The problems Vermont faced weren't all that bad, not compared with police brutality or voter suppression or—well, a lot of things. And wouldn't those get worse if the Vermonts of the country just walked away? Hell, left to its own devices,

Wyoming might turn Yellowstone into a geothermal power plant. Vern's world still worked—he just wasn't all that fond of it. And he didn't think the center could hold that much longer. But people always thought that, and for about 240 years the country had staggered on. Sometimes the country had *surged* on—certainly in his youth. Maybe it was all foolishness.

Maybe it was worse than that, he thought—maybe it was mostly ego. He'd long known he liked listening to himself talk, liked the cadence and the artful pause, liked the ability to sound folksy, though the minute you started thinking about sounding folksy it was obviously a fake, Garth Brooks instead of Jimmie Rodgers. Or maybe Garth Brooks was real, in his own mind. But *he* wasn't entirely real, he knew. He knew he liked attention, some part of him liked it too much—he knew he was showing off, and it scared him a little. Because if you showed off when you were leading people, you could lead them right over an edge. But slowing down now, backing off now, would be—embarrassing. Real politicians didn't do doubt; decades of interviewing had taught him that much. Sure, selectmen, and maybe even state legislators, who after all were just part-timers, heading back home to their law offices or their farms when the session ended each April; they actually weighed arguments, and changed their minds. But not governors—they stayed on message, they talked right through objections, they communicated clarity and confidence.

He could do it too—he'd been doing it for the past six weeks, one podcast after another, and he'd enjoyed it; it felt good to lead, to imagine every ear turned in your direction. But he didn't really believe it, or believe in it. It felt like acting, and he felt like an actor. He knew precisely how fallible he was—he sensed he was on the right path, he really did think the country was too big, out of control. But it was one thing to argue that, and another to act on it, and the pleasure he took made him all the more suspicious. *He had burned down someone's house*, more or less. There'd been *guns*, people firing guns. Guns didn't scare him—he'd been around them all his life. People firing fusillades at what they assumed was him—that scared him. Not because he didn't want to get shot—he didn't particularly, but he was an old man. Because anyone believing anything strongly enough to pull a trigger for it scared him. It ran contrary to everything he'd ever wanted to do, which was mostly to talk calmly about things, with his neighbors, maybe in a little bit more folksy way than was actually quite real. But when you did it long enough it became real.

"Perry," he said. "I don't know how you're going to do it, but this time we really do need to set it up so we can talk to people. So they can call in and say something on the radio and I can talk back to them. Can talk *with* them. Can listen to them talk."

Perry had been quietly reading a magazine article to Martha Oxbow. "I've been thinking it through, and we can do it, I think," he said, laying down the magazine. "It will be a little weird," he said after a pause. "But I think we can manage.

We'll listen to the radio here, and when someone calls in we'll hear it, and you'll answer into the microphone, which we'll put on Skype to a friend I have in Colorado? And she'll phone the signal back to the radio station? It's not foolproof—the police will eventually be able to track down where the phone line is coming from, and if they found her while we were still live I guess they could conceivably track the Skype call back here. But we'll make sure she's someplace public—some payphone, if they still have them out there. I don't see how they could trace it in less than half an hour anyway, and that's all you want, right?"

"That's all I want, that's plenty," said Vern. "We'll have to tell Mark to turn off the seven-second delay. The FCC won't like that—but then, the FCC won't like any of this. Someone saying a bad word will be the least of our worries."

"I'll get to work," said Perry. "You finish this magazine article, okay?"

25

As usual, Vern grew steadily calmer as the minute hand moved toward the top of the hour. They were listening to WDEV on Martha Oxbow's table radio, and Perry was monitoring the Skype connection to Colorado Springs. Mark Johnson was paying the station's bills, offering his testimonials to some of the small businesses that still could afford to advertise. "The Greensboro Garage—if they can't fix your Subaru, you might as well buy a new one," he said. "It's seven p.m., and as most of you know, we've got an old friend on the show tonight. I grew up listening to Vern Barclay, and he's one reason I'm in this business. We'd welcome him to these airwaves anytime, but right now he's also the most wanted man in the State of Vermont. In fact, Vern, I should probably tell you that there are a couple of federal agents here in the studio with me tracing the phone line. I couldn't stop them—they have a warrant—but I told them they couldn't stop me from talking about it. I have a warrant too, and it's the First Amendment."

"That's okay, Mark. Those men have a job to do. And I've got a job to do tonight as well, which is to listen to Vermonters. If I'm remembering correctly from all my years of listening to your show, the number if you're in central Vermont is 244-1777, or across the state at 877-291-TALK. Since I'm not there in the studio with you, and since the governor has been insisting I'm now beyond the veil, some listeners might worry that this is just a tape recording of a dead man. So let me begin by saying it's Thursday, February twenty-eighth, and congratulations to the Windsor girls for their big win in last night's state semifinal against Montpelier—Tracy Ingersoll, twenty-two points in the second half. But the big news comes from the National Weather Service, which is predicting that tomorrow will bring the first serious snowstorm in three years to the Green Mountain State. An Alberta Clipper pouring cold air down from the Canadian prairies will combine with a rapidly deepening offshore low to set up what forecasters are calling a 'major snow event,' thirty-six hours of blizzard that could leave parts of the state with up to two and a half feet of snow. Time to find that shovel buried in the back of the garage, folks, and if you've got kids who've never seen a real Vermont storm, it's time to dig that sled out of the attic. It's going to be a good one.

"But the snowstorm's not all that's coming our way. Town Meeting Day is next Tuesday, and I know many towns get started the night before—along with all the regular items on the docket, 231 of Vermont's 246 cities and towns will be debating the question: 'Should the legislature be instructed to study the state's possible secession from the United States?' Two nights earlier, on Saturday, as you've doubtless heard, the governor is hosting a 'Celebration of America' at the fine new Bruce Facility, arguing that the answer should be no. Tonight I'll try to suggest why a better answer might be yes—why you might want to at least consider a free and independent nation of Vermont. But I'm not going to do more than suggest, because I'm not certain I'm right—for decades I've learned what I've needed to know from listening to you. Mark, is there a caller on the line?"

"Every line is full," came the reply over the table radio. "First caller is Sue from Alburgh."

"Hi, Mark. Hi, Vern. My question is, When you have a country of Vermont, are you going to let there be the greyhound racing like they have in Massachusetts? Because I think it's cruel, and I wouldn't want to see it here."

"Thank you, Sue. I tend to agree with you about the puppy track—there's something about chasing that mechanical rabbit that's just depressing. But here's the point I need to make right at the beginning. I have *no, none,* not the *slightest* interest in running Vermont. I'm not suited for running anything more powerful than a radio switchboard; if a free Vermont came with me attached, I'd vote against it at town meeting and advise everyone else to do the same. And don't support it thinking that you'll necessarily get a better class of politicians—I mean, Vermonters elected the current governor six times. The only advantage, as I see it, is that at least you'll have the chance to make decisions about things that matter—greyhound racing, but also whether or not to give health care to everyone, and if we should subsidize big farms or little ones, and if we want to send our daughters and sons off to fight. Right now those decisions are made so far away that it's almost impossible to really influence them. A few years ago the Supreme Court said that corporations were persons, and so they could spend any amount of money they wanted on elections; if the spirit of Jefferson was still alive, that was the day they put him in the ICU. Vermont by itself wouldn't be perfect—but it would be smaller. So we could actually see what was going on."

"Vern, we've got Ed on line two, from Ferrisburgh."

Vern was sitting in his straight-backed chair, feet planted wide, hunched over on his elbows, eyes closed. He felt entirely relaxed, at ease, in the flow—the same feeling he'd always had when he strapped on a pair of skis and headed out onto the snow. He wondered idly if he'd spent more of his life in front of the microphone or in the woods.

"Hi there, this is Ed. I get the corporations thing, but I don't want to lose my constitutional guarantees."

"Which ones in particular?"

"Guns. The Second Amendment. My right to bear arms."

"Well, then, you'll be glad to know that the U.S. Constitution is not the only one in the world. Vermont's constitution predates it by some years. It's the shortest of all the state constitutions, and it *begins* with a Bill of Rights. Article Sixteen, if I'm remembering correctly, is guns: 'The people have a right to bear arms for the defense of themselves and the state.' That's about as straightforward as it gets. But it adds something interesting: 'As standing armies in times of peace are dangerous to liberty, they ought not to be kept up.' That seems smarter all the time to me, given the difficulties standing armies seem to keep getting us into. If we'd had to go out and raise an army to invade Iraq, we might have thought a little harder. We're used to thinking that the U.S. Constitution is the greatest single document ever devised, but it's worth remembering it was mostly set up to keep things from happening, because the states were suspicious of each other. Small states check big states, and so on. Good idea, except we're pretty well checkmated right now."

"Vern, Mark here. I think I need to tell you that the *federales* here seem to be making progress—they just started shouting into their cell phones out there in the control room."

"Mark, thanks for the warning. Don't worry, though—I'm going to turn myself in right after Town Meeting Day anyway. I figure that if I have to spend my time hidden away indoors, I can probably do it as easily in the jail as in a room like this one. I'd just like to stay on the loose a few more days so we can keep this conversation alive. Speaking of which, do you have another caller?"

"This is Marsha, from Clarendon. And I don't, like, trust politicians? I voted for Obama and then nothing changed. And I've never been to town meeting because it's not for people like me. So I just mostly concentrate on my family."

"Marsha, just do me one favor. Go to town meeting on Tuesday. I think Clarendon meets in the town hall, next to the church. You don't have to say anything, just sit there and listen. We all need to be reminded that democracy isn't just voting for president every four years and then trusting him to fix things. Democracy is about getting together with your community to think together about your future. Sometimes it's dull, and sometimes people get long-winded, and sometimes they get stiff-necked. But town meeting has been going for three hundred years, ever since people got to Vermont. Just go see."

Vern felt a tap on his shoulder and opened his eyes—Perry was signaling him to wrap up.

"Mark, just time for one more caller here, and even that may be pressing our luck."

"This is Art from Essex Junction. I just want to say, I think this whole thing is so stupid. The U.S. is the greatest country on earth. If we were off by ourselves, we'd be crushed. We'd be Haiti with Holsteins. That's it—just stupid."

"Ed, thanks for the call. And it's the right note to end on. Because I think you're wrong—I think we'd be more like

Finland with fall colors. I think we've got plenty of brains and resources to do just fine on our own. But you may be right. And that's the point. I've sat behind a microphone and listened for decades as Americans learned to stop talking with each other and start shouting instead. No discussions, just 'socialist' or 'fascist' or 'feminazi' or 'bigot' or whatever. So here's what I want to say, and I think it's the one thing no one ever says anymore in our public life: I think you're wrong, but *you may be right*."

Perry was slashing his index finger across his throat with ever greater vigor. Vern didn't let himself speed up—he may even have slowed down a little just to be sure he didn't sound panicked. "Folks, go to town meeting on Tuesday, and listen to each other. Pay attention to the people you trust, listen to their arguments. This is a big question, and we want to get it right, and the only way we will is if we all think it through. Many thanks for being with us tonight, and remember, there's a big snowstorm on the way. Don't drive if you can help it— ski instead! Mark, thank you for—"

At that moment Perry pulled the cord from the modem. "We're shut down," he said. "Sorry, but they were closing in. Your computer was skyped into a desktop in Colorado, and my friend was talking to me from across the street. She could see the agents coming; she had a button to press that fries the hard drive. They might be able to figure out where we were coming from, but not very fast I don't think."

"Don't worry," said Vern. "We've said our piece. Nothing

to do now but sit and wait till Tuesday." He picked up the magazine and began to read to Martha Oxbow. But he'd covered barely a paragraph when the door blew open, and his mother stormed in as fast as her walker would allow.

"Mom," said Vern. "Did you hear the radio?"

"Thought you sounded a little wussy, like you wanted everyone to like you," she said. "But it doesn't matter. We've got bigger problems. They got Trance."

"What? Where?"

"It's my fault. She was going crazy aquacising. It's like running in slow motion, she said. So we fixed her up so she could go out for a proper run. She didn't look anything like herself—hair, clothes. I mean, she was wearing a pink sweat suit—I don't think Trance ever wore pink once in her life. But she hadn't gone two blocks when a car almost rammed her. She went right over the hood—we could see it from the dayroom window. She got up but they tackled her, two men in suits, and they tossed her in the back of the car. It was black. I have no idea how they knew it was her."

"They knew it was her because she's the only woman in Vermont who can run a fifteen-minute five-K. Her hair's not what gives her away—it's her stride."

"Well, it's my fault," said her mother, sniffling. "I like her so much, and she was going crazy with nothing to do. And she was missing that Sylvia."

"No one ever really told Trance not to do something," said

Vern. "Do you think they saw her come out of the door of the home? She won't give us away, but maybe they saw her."

"If they'd seen her, they'd be here by now," said Perry.

"Oh Christ," said Vern. "I don't even like to think about what they're doing to her to find out. You remember how I said a few minutes ago on the radio that we should all just be friends and talk things through and all that?"

"I do," said Perry.

"Well," said Vern. "To hell with that. This is more like war. We're going to get her free, and we're going to do it no matter what."

26

Trance was lying on the floor of the backseat of a car, her hands cuffed behind, a blanket over her head, and the feet of her captor resting on the small of her back. She'd struggled for a minute when they'd pushed her into the car, but one of the men had shown her the gun he carried, a standard government-issue Glock 22.

"I'm no sniper, Trance. On the other hand, I'm three feet away, so I don't think I'll miss."

She'd relaxed, lain down, and begun to think. It had happened fast—she'd run barely three blocks, not enough to get her breathing hard, before the car had pulled across her path and she'd gone over the hood. Had they known she was there, or was it a lucky break?

"Didn't think we'd find you today," said the man, as if he could read her mind. "But I'm glad we did. We've got some work for you to do."

"Where are you taking me?" she asked.

"Somewhere safe and secure," he said. He spoke with a flat, clipped accent—midwestern, the law-enforcement default since the days of Hoover.

Trance had felt the car accelerate onto the highway, and she felt it exit again about twenty minutes later. Since Vermont had exactly one highway, that meant they'd either gone south to somewhere near Randolph, or north to somewhere near Bolton. She was paying attention even though the agent was keeping up a steady stream of talk on his radio, milking her catch for all it was worth with his superiors.

"Yes sir, we'd been paying close attention to her possible whereabouts. But it was some luck that we found her . . . Yes sir, well, maybe some skill as well, thank you, sir . . . Yes sir, Psy Ops command, at Alpha HQ. On the way, we'll be there in half an hour."

This guy is not too bright, thought Trance. *He has a Glock, which ups his IQ about forty points, but he's got an ego, which probably knocks it down about the same. Just pay attention,* she told herself. *This isn't good, but they clearly don't know where Vern and Perry are yet.*

The car twisted through some mountain corners, and came to a brief stop at a gate of some kind, where the driver simply said, "Whitestream Security," and got a grunt in return. They drove a few more minutes, and then stopped. The agent with the Glock draped the blanket over her head and lifted her from the car, squeezing her obliques a little more than he needed to in the process. He led her inside and through a hallway, depositing her on a folding chair before taking off the blanket.

Trance took a look around. The room was nondescript—a light green wall, a bookshelf, an American flag, a picture of the president. She knew instantly where she was, right down to the square meter. No need to have counted minutes on the freeway—this was an upstairs room in the barracks at the Ethan Allen Firing Range, Vermont's only real military facility. More to the point, it was the place where America's biathletes came to train—she'd spent every summer of her girlhood roller-skiing on the concrete track that ran through the woods, and she'd raced here a dozen times a winter. The year she'd gone to the Olympics, this was where she'd raced the qualifier, blazing through the course she knew like the back of her hand. Yes, she thought, these guys were none too bright. They might as well have brought her to her mother's kitchen. But she looked around, blinking, pretending she hadn't seen this very room a hundred times before—in biathlon season it was where they put the massage tables, rubbed away the lactic acid that gathered in calf and quad. She'd lain on her stomach and stared at this same flag, this same presidential portrait, albeit with a different face. She felt at home, as at home as you could be when your hands were cuffed and a man sat on the other side of the desk idly fingering a very powerful handgun.

"Where am I?"

"You're in a very secure place, that's all you need to know," the man said. "That, and that if you cooperate nothing will happen."

"Am I under arrest?" she asked. "Do I need a lawyer?"

"Like your friend Sylvia? Maybe she can spare you one of her posse? No, we don't arrest traitors. You're an . . . enemy combatant. And frankly, everyone thinks you're dead, which means we can do pretty much what we'd like with you. I mean, it's not like you could die again, is it?" He smiled.

You're showing off, Trance thought. But she didn't say anything.

The door opened, and another man walked in, this one in a blue shirt and yellow tie with an open Kevlar vest that said "Whitestream" front and back. "Hi, Dave," he said. "And this would be our new friend?"

"Chet, meet Trance Harper. Olympic gold medalist, renowned sharpshooter, and traitor to her country. Trance, Chet is a psychological specialist—he can help deprogram you." Trance just looked at the two of them and didn't even bother shaking her head.

"Dave, why don't you leave us alone for a few minutes so the two of us can get better acquainted?" said Chet. He pulled his Glock out of the vest while Dave picked his up and walked from the room.

"Sorry for Dave," he said once the door had closed. "Psychologically speaking, he's a little overexcited. You're a big catch!"

I hope they've got the bright ones out doing something important, Trance thought.

"Now, Trance, we need you to do a little assignment for us, just make a little video to help us out," he said.

She looked at him steadily, without saying a word, which seemed to disconcert him, because he began to talk a little faster.

"Just a short video. Not a long video. Just a few minutes. It says in your profile that you don't like to talk in public. I get that. I didn't like to speak in public either, till I joined Toastmasters International, which I recommend. But this will be easy. We'll give you a script. You can add your own words if you want, but you don't need to—you can just read off the paper."

Trance stared at him a minute more, and finally said: "Why?"

"What do you mean, 'Why?'"

"I mean, why should I? I went for a run, your friend Dave tackled me and put me in a car at gunpoint, and brought me here to . . . some mysterious place. Why should I help you?"

Chet thought for a moment, as if the question hadn't really occurred to him before. "I guess because—well, I guess because we'll shoot you if you don't."

That's the first smart thing anyone's said since I got here, Trance thought. Not exactly Psy Ops, but persuasive. She looked up at the man and said: "Okay."

~~~

Mrs. Barclay sat on the bed, watching TV with her silent friend. "I've got a Big Butt, but you don't see me Working It," she said. "What's wrong with these people, Martha?"

Vern and Perry sat at the desk, making a series of phone calls to reporters—Perry had set up a new skein of VoIP lines, and he figured they were probably safe if they didn't talk too long. "It doesn't matter anyway," said Vern. "Trance isn't safe, not until we get the word out that they have her. Right now they can do anything they want with her—she might as well be at Guantánamo."

"Hello, Louis?" he said. "Vern Barclay . . . Yeah, thanks, I thought it went well too . . . Look, they've got Trance, they got her last night, off the street in Montpelier . . . No, I don't know who 'they' is, some kind of fed . . . Louis, you're the reporter, that's why I'm calling you."

"Will he write a story?" asked Perry.

"We don't have much for him to go on," said Vern. "A call from someone saying he's Vern Barclay telling him Trance Harper has been kidnapped by an unknown someone in a black car. But we don't actually need him to *write* the story, we just need a few of them calling the authorities to check it out. Just so they know they can't disappear her no questions asked."

"I don't think you need to worry about that," said Mrs. Barclay. "In fact, I think you better come watch the news."

Their old friend Horace LaRossette was standing on the Church Street Mall in Burlington, lazy flakes of snow softly dropping around him. "Two big stories this evening in Vermont," he said. "First, snow has begun to fall, and our Channel 3 YouCrew WeatherWatchers team is warning this will be the real thing. And fugitive Trance Harper has turned up alive—and not only that, she's *turned*. Here's a videotape just released by state authorities, exclusively to WVTV."

Trance's face filled the screen. She looked tired and tense, but fine. She began to talk, glancing down regularly at the paper in front of her.

"Hello, Vermonters," she read, in the wooden tone she reserved for public speaking. "I would like to thank you all for your support and prayers. I am sure that they helped me escape unharmed from the terrorists that have been holding me. Those terrorists made me say things I did not believe, and ma—malign the country that I love. They are very dangerous and I hope they will be captured soon so their reign of terror will cease. They have misled many Vermonters into supporting their call for an independent Vermont, but I know any of you who go to town meeting next week will do the right thing and vote against terrorism. I hope many of you will join me and the governor tomorrow at the new retractable-roof facility off Exit Fourteen in Burlington for the Salute to America at six p.m."

Trance looked down at her papers, and then up at the camera, suddenly speaking with more animation. "I've spent my whole life in Vermont, and I love the whole state: from Underhill to Richmond, from Jericho to Bolton, and everywhere in between, along all the paths and trails of my girlhood. Please join me in helping to protect this place from, uh, terrorism. And thank you again for all your prayers."

The screen flashed back to Horace—the snow was falling fast enough that it had begun to accumulate on the shoulders of his trench coat. "Last night it was Vern Barclay on the radio, and today Trance Harper on video—it seems safe to say they survived the shootout at their hiding place that we carried exclusively on Channel 3, but it also seems safe to say that their terror cell is breaking apart. We'll have more reaction later, but first let's switch to the Channel 3 Extreme Weather Center Emergency Desk, where Kitty Clarkson will have today's Channel 3 Youcast so You can plan Your day."

Kitty was pointing to a radar map that showed the entire Northeast about to be swallowed by a gaping maw of cloud, but Vern took the clicker and muted the sound. "At least we know she's safe, and at least we know where she is—now we can go to work," he said.

"What do you mean, 'know where she is'?" asked Perry.

"She sent a pretty strong signal," said Vern. "Underhill and Jericho and Bolton and Richmond aren't actually the 'whole State of Vermont.' In fact, they border each other, and in the middle is the exact place where Trance Harper spent half her life, the Ethan Allen Firing Range, where the National Guard has let the biathlon team train since before my time. For Vermont it's pretty well guarded, but it's still four-teen thousand acres, most of it woods. We'll get her out—we've just got to start rounding up the right people."

He went to the window and opened the curtain a bit—in the dusk, snow was coming down hard. It looked like the flakes were hurrying to get out of the sky so the next ones would have room to fall. He'd never in his life watched the snow come down without feeling unreasonably giddy—the world turning itself slippery and white and quiet and fast. And tonight it felt especially sweet. On their own, he figured he and his friends probably weren't much of a match for the feds. But the feds hadn't spent half their lives on skis. He re-membered skiing in Oslo in the early '60s, after some kind of world junior championship. He'd stayed on a few days, criss-crossing the trails in the Oslomarka at the edge of town and one day he'd fallen into an easy stride behind an older man. When he stopped to drink some water, Vern stopped with him, and found that he knew a little English from his days in the Resistance. The Americans had dropped weapons from airplanes far back in the woods, he said, and all winter long the skiers had hauled them back to the farmhouses on the edge of town.

"The Germans owned the cities," the man said. "But the Germans—the Germans can't really ski. So we owned every-where else."

27

Six men were gathered in the parking lot of the On the Rise Bakery in Richmond when Vern and Perry pulled in, fishtailing in the heavy snow; at least a foot had fallen overnight, and the storm was deepening. The men were eating fresh bagels and scones—they held out the sack as Vern and Perry stepped out into the cold.

"Coach."

"Hey, Coach."

"Good to see you, Coach."

"Good to see you boys, and thanks for coming," said Vern.

"I was glad you called," said one, who was sitting on the hood of a Subaru. "Once I listened to Trance give that roadmap, I was about to round up the boys and see what we could do."

"Let's hope they didn't figure out what she was doing," said Vern. "Perry, this is Mike, and Mike, and that over there is Mike too, though we call him Replay, on account of he shoots like a dream but skis in slow motion."

"Much faster now that I've retired and gone on an all-scone diet," he said.

"I'm sure," said Vern. "And this is Steve, and Burke, and Gardner. Guys, this is Perry. Doesn't ski, but he does something better. Computers."

"And music," said Gardner. "I've got your compilation CD on my iPod. I play it when I work out."

"Thanks," said Perry. "Maybe I should go," he added, nervous to be standing out in the open for the first time in weeks, even though the visibility was down to a dozen feet at best.

"Drive carefully," said Vern. "Stick in the right lane of the Interstate, and stay at forty, and you'll be okay. When you get to the university, go where I told you in the journalism building. There'll be a door open, and a phone ready to use, and an actual fast Internet. Don't worry too much about them tracing your calls—I think we're going to be giving them enough to worry about today."

Before Perry left, Vern pulled eight squat rifles from the trunk of the car and handed them out.

"I've got my gun with me," said Burke. "What the heck is this thing?"

"These things shoot rubber bullets," said Vern. "The Montpelier police use them for crowd control, and a friend of mine borrowed them this morning from the storage locker.

Hopefully the day will pass without any riots and they'll never know they're missing."

The men were examining the weapons curiously—sighting, playing with safeties. "These are ugly," said Burke. "Why aren't we using our regular rifles?"

"Well," said Vern, "because I really don't want you guys shooting actual bullets at federal officers. That's a serious crime, the kind that lets you sit in prison for forty years. And I don't think it will do our little movement much good either— shooting never seems to help, as the governor found out when they blew up that house in Starksboro."

"Yeah, were you staying in that house or what?" asked Replay.

"Not important," said Vern. "What's important is, the rubber bullets these things fire are about the size of a roll-on deodorant. Now, the feds will be on snowmobiles—Arctic Cat X-700s to be precise. Since they're military, they don't have any environmental regs to follow, none of those fancy silencing mufflers. Just the old-fashioned twin pipes. And our old friend Lou at L. C. Greenwood and Sons assures me that one of these rubber bullets plugging one half of the exhaust should be enough to bring it to a halt while they flood the engine. Get both pipes and it's a guarantee."

"How accurate are these things?" asked one of the Mikes.

"Not accurate at all," said Vern. "They're designed to be fired into a crowd of protesters from forty yards away if you don't care which protester you hit. You're going to have to be *close* to the snowmobile if you want to have a chance. And here's the thing—they're going to be firing at you, and I'm pretty sure they're going to be using real ammunition. This isn't like biathlon—your targets never shot back. So you have to be careful. And quick. But you always were quick."

"Except for Replay," said Burke.

"Now with scone power," he replied.

The men, in two Subaru station wagons with ski pods on the roof, followed a plow most of the way to the firing range. Vern sat in the backseat of one, cap pulled low over his brow. When they got to the first gate, Mike opened his window and leaned out.

"Hi, Howie," he said. "How about this snow? First chance to practice all season."

"Hi, boys—you go on in, but they're closing the whole place down in two hours—snow emergency," the fellow said. "Did you see Trance on TV yesterday? I'm glad she's okay."

They drove another mile or two on the entrance drive, till they were near the more heavily guarded interior gate, and then they stashed the vehicles behind a storage shed, and pulled on ski boots.

"Blue wax day," said Vern, handing around a little canister of the stuff that lets skis stick on the uphills and slide on the downs. "Temperature won't get above twenty-five, and this snow couldn't be fresher. Here's the plan, such as it is. I'm pretty sure they've got her up in the conference rooms above the main barracks—they'll wait up there till it's time to go down to the governor's shindig. We'll go up the main trail till we see trouble, and then you guys split in three pairs and try to keep them occupied. I'm not carrying a weapon—I'm going to put Trance's skis on my back so she'll have some way to get out of there fast."

"Frontal assault?" said Steve. "You don't want to take the back trails?"

"I'm guessing they're not expecting us, and I'm guessing our disguise might get us most of the way there," said Vern. "I mean, we sort of look like a ski team." All seven had stripped down to green spandex tops, with a map of Vermont in gold across the chest. The other six took out their rifle slings, and replaced their light and accurate biathlon rifles with the police weaponry, which looked like toys by comparison. Vern stuck on a knapsack, with side straps to keep Trance's skis in place, and the seven of them struck out along the road. The snow was so deep already that skiing would have been hard work except for the set of tire tracks from some truck that had driven in perhaps an hour earlier. Two inches of snow had fallen since, but the track made a solid enough base to keep the skiing fast. They naturally formed two lines, three in one and four in the other, and set off at an easy tempo.

Easy for six of them, anyway, who were only a few years from high-level competition. A stiff pace for Vern, who was in his seventies and hadn't moved in weeks. But the sheer pleasure of skiing made up for the tightness in his chest—they kicked forward more or less in unison, a fourteen-legged animal covering ground fast, with only the quiet hiss of ski on snow and the small clouds of breath to mark their passage. *It's all about efficiency,* Vern kept reminding himself—it was always his mantra for the first ski of the year. As much glide from every push as you can get. No friction.

But gravity still applied, and the hill began to steepen as they approached the second, interior fence, this one topped with concertina wire. There was another gate, and they could see the guard in the small shack watching them with growing curiosity as they kept their steady pace in his direction. "Just keep going," puffed Vern. "Don't even slow down." The guard came out of his hut to talk as they approached, but without breaking stride they crouched, their momentum letting them glide under the stop barrier, and then resumed their stride on the other side.

"Hey," the guard shouted, and then he grabbed his rifle—but he hesitated. He'd doubtless been told, thought Vern, that this was where the Olympians trained; you wouldn't want to shoot an athlete. He could hear the guard yelling into a radio instead. They all could hear him—and the pace picked up, still relaxed enough to be efficient, but now Vern could really feel his heart start to pound.

"You okay, Coach?" asked Gardner over his shoulder.

"Of course I am," said Vern, who would have much sooner suffered a massive coronary than suggest slowing the pace. "Just a little out of training."

The road had been plowed sometime during the night, and snowbanks hemmed them in on either side. Over the pounding of his heart, Vern could hear the whine of snowmobiles starting not far ahead. "As soon as you can see those sleds, split up and take them on a chase," he said, straining so they wouldn't hear him pant. "I'm hiding behind that shed and hoping the snowstorm will keep them from counting." He jumped the snowbank, and glided to a stop beside a small outbuilding in a little grove of red pines.

Through the scrim of falling, blowing flakes, he could see the six men powering up the road, and he could see the snowmobiles roaring down the road. He strained to count them: four machines, damn. The line of skiers began to split: Mike and Mike jumped the bank and headed left, toward the top of the biathlon course. Steve and Replay went right, headed toward a beech woods where the brown leaves still hung in tatters. Burke and Gardner just reversed course, plunging back down the road till they were past his shed, then hanging a left out across the open field. Two of the black snow machines followed them, one each on the other pairs, and now Vern could see that there were two men on each of the sleds, in black uniforms with helmets. No rifles strapped to their backs, but he was pretty confident there were handguns in easy reach, and they were gaining fast.

No time to worry, he thought. He skied through the deep snow and then back out onto the main track, racing now as hard as he could. It didn't look hard—it never did, which is why when they showed the Winter Olympics all you got was about forty seconds of Nordic skiing for every six hours of ice dancing. But at full speed there was no more aerobic activity on earth: arms and legs both cranking hard, stomach muscles flexing with every pole plant. The snowmobiles had made the track harder, faster; he hadn't raced in many years, but he could feel himself redlining as he crested the hill with the barracks appearing out of the snow in front of him.

Remember, he told himself, *pace yourself coming into the range.* He wasn't going to have to shoot, but he would definitely need to think—he slowed a little over the last hundred yards, letting his heart rate fall, and he slid to a stop by the fire escape on the west end of the building. He pulled off his skis, and slid Trance's from the pack straps, sticking both pairs tail-end down in the snowbank.

The fire escape ran straight to the ground—this wasn't like the city, where they were worried about thieves—and he trotted up two flights. The door he wanted was, as expected, locked. So he climbed over the railing of the fire escape, aiming for the short leap to the nearest window. The sill was just as he'd remembered, a good eight inches wide. But the five-foot jump looked longer than it had when he'd done it dozens of times in his youth, this being the way young biathletes snuck in and out of their training camp to drink beer. It's true that there was a good eighteen inches of fresh snow on the ground, but it was also true that the ground was twenty feet below, and that bones of his vintage tended to be brittle.

He hesitated, and then heard the snarl of the snow machines in the distance, and a shot. Compared to the chance those guys were taking . . .

He leaped, and landed on both feet on the sill, grabbing the top of the window as his ski boots slid. It wasn't exactly stealthy, he thought. If anyone was actually in the room, they were looking out at a green spandex torso splayed across the center of the pane, almost like those cardboard targets the FBI practiced on in every TV movie he'd ever watched. He clung there a moment, catching his breath. He took the fact that nobody shot him as a good sign, and cautiously lowered his head to look inside. And there was Trance, giggling.

She pointed to her feet to show they were cuffed to a chair, but then mimed lifting the window. Vern did, and found it unlocked. He slipped inside as quietly as he could, closed it behind him, and then turned around to give Trance a hug.

"Thought you might show up," she said. "Actually, I thought you might send someone younger."

"Everyone younger is out playing hide-and-go-seek with unpleasant men on snowmobiles," he said. "Let's get you out of here so you can play too. Where are the keys to these cuffs?"

"Agent Dave's got them in his pants pocket," said Trance. "Dave, could you come in here?" she said, loudly.

"Wha—what?" said Vern.

"Sure, honey, I'll be right in," came a voice from down the

hall, followed shortly by someone who looked like a wannabe FBI agent dressing down for a big snowstorm. He was carrying a gun, but he didn't tighten his grip on it till he saw Vern standing next to Trance.

"Who are you?" he asked, raising the Glock to cover them both.

"Dave, meet Vern Barclay. He's a terrorist."

"Vern . . . I've caught both of you?" said Dave.

"Both of us, yeah," said Trance. "Now give me the key to cuffs that you've got in your pocket."

"The key—you think just because you've handed me your terrorist pal I'm going to let you go? I'm bringing both of you in. This will make me."

"Dave's ambitious," said Trance to Vern, who was trying not to shake. "A go-getter." Dave had been getting closer, and reaching toward his belt for another pair of handcuffs. But as soon as he was inside of three feet Trance simply reached out, grabbed the barrel of the gun, and pulled it out of his hands. She turned it on him and said, "Get down." Which he did, quickly.

Vern got the keys from his pocket, unlocked them from around Trance's feet, and put them on Dave's wrists. "Trance, weren't you just a little worried he'd shoot you?" he asked. "I was a little worried, right about the moment you grabbed the barrel of his gun."

"Not too worried," she said. "Dave was feeling frisky last night, and he put his very sophisticated big-city moves on me.

Right about the moment he was trying to unhook my sports bra—which, by the way, Dave, for future reference sports bras don't have hooks—I was removing the magazine from his Glock. It's still here, in my bra, in fact, for safekeeping."

"Wait, this guy was trying to kiss you while you were *cuffed?*" said Vern.

"I think that might have made it better for him," said Trance. "You remember how I told you I like girls? Sometimes I think I just don't like boys. Present company excepted."

"And the six guys out there getting shot at—let's go," said Vern, handing her a pair of ski boots from the pack.

But suddenly Dave, who'd been blushing, yelled, "Chet! Help!"

They heard a door open down the hall. "Who's Chet?" asked Vern.

"Agent Chet," said Trance. "Psy Ops. Perhaps you could stand behind the door with this," she said, handing him the Glock. Vern moved back by the jamb, just as Chet burst through, looking bewildered at the sight of Dave on the floor in handcuffs.

"Hi, Chet," said Trance. "Could you please kneel down on the floor next to Dave?"

"Why should I?" he asked.

"Because Vern will shoot you if you don't," she said, pointing with her eyes. Chet glanced backward, saw the man with the gun, and began to sink.

"No!" said Dave. "It's not loaded. The clip is in—it's in

her bra. Take your gun out of your holster and shoot these guys!"

Chet looked around at the three of them.

"This is an interesting moment for a psychological specialist like yourself," said Trance. "Dave says the gun is unloaded, and the clip is in my brassiere. That's possible, I suppose. You know Dave well. If you trust his judgment, then you should probably take your gun out your holster and shoot us. If not, I'd be grateful if you'd kneel right there."

Chet looked around again. Then he sank to his knees.

"My opinion exactly," said Trance. She cuffed him back-to-back with Dave, then took the gun from Vern and put it on the floor just out of their reach. "Though in this case, he was actually making sense." She pulled the clip from her chest, and laid it on the desk. "I'll let Dave tell you the whole story—in fact, it will probably prove psychologically interesting. And then you guys can figure out how to explain why my fingerprints are all over your guns and your bullets."

She finished lacing on the boots. "Vern, I bet you brought me some gloves and a hat too," she said.

"Of course," he said. "And your Green Mountain ski shirt, so you'll look like the rest of us." He turned around to let her put it on.

"Maybe we should take one of these federal badges in case it comes in handy later," she said. "Oh, and Vern, do you have room in that knapsack for Dave's laptop? I think Perry might find something interesting in there."

"Plenty of room, but you may have to carry it," said Vern. "I was having . . . just a little trouble keeping up with the boys up the last hill."

"No problem," said Trance. "And thanks for coming. I'd been wanting a ski ever since that snow started to fall."

The pair ran down the fire escape stairs and clicked into their skis. The snow was falling, if anything, harder. They were headed downhill and picking up speed, which meant they couldn't see much—the snow was whipping their faces. But fifteen yards in front of them a snowmobile suddenly went airborne right to left, jumping off the snowbank on one side of the lane and landing past the bank on the other. The driver was hunched over the wheel, but behind him his part-ner was gripping the seat with his knees and firing rapidly. Ten seconds behind him, another snowmobile cleared the bank—this one with three guys in green on board. One was driving, the next had his back to the driver and his arms around the waist of the third, who was kneeling with an odd-looking gun to his shoulder. "That looked like Mike and Mike—and Replay?" yelled Trance.

"It sure is," said another voice—Trance looked over her shoulder to see Steve and Burke and Gardner dropping in line behind them on skis, tucking down the hill. "I've got no idea what the feds are shooting at anymore, and I don't think they do either," said Steve. "This isn't like biathlon—no pen-alty if you miss, so shoot all you want."

"Where are the other agents?" shouted Vern.

"Wandering around in the woods," Burke shouted back. "Those machines are fast as hell, but they're not much at tight turns. Number one hit a beech tree, and number two hit a birch—and once they were off their horses, the jockeys couldn't move much in this snow. I think 'floundering' would be the technical term. That's how those three got a snow machine of their own. And since Mike used to groom trails, he actually knows how to drive it."

Up ahead they could see the black snowmobile, its crew still firing wildly, and the three Vermonters about twenty yards behind, with Replay trying to line up a shot. He waited till they were on flat ground, then carefully squeezed once. The rubber bullet was fat and beige, and traveled slowly enough that they could actually watch its flight—in fact, it hardly went faster than the speeding snowmobile. Slowly, slowly—but it plunked home into the left exhaust.

"Bull's-eye," said Burke. "That's a tough shot."

The fed sled coughed and stammered for a few seconds, and then quit—and with its engine suddenly silent, the agents could hear the roar of the other snowmobile as it banked hard and headed for the road. They fired a few shots in its direction, but Mike angled it off the snowbank and back into the middle of the road—now his machine was leading the five skiers down the hill, and back toward the gate they'd rushed maybe fifteen minutes before. This time the guard was facing their way, gun drawn.

"Stop," he yelled.

Mike responded by revving the engine one notch higher with a twist of his wrist. He sunk down behind the windshield as they drove straight for the guard, who let off one panicked round and then dove for the bank, just in time. The snow-mobile crashed through the stop barrier with the skiers about ten yards behind, all still in formation but now whooping— their momentum carried them the half mile to where the cars were parked behind the shed. The three climbed off the snowmobile, and there were hugs all around for Trance, who did her best to look tough.

"Thanks, guys," she said. "Replay, nice shot."

"The scones settled me," he said. "You need some ballast for a shot like that."

"Should we pile in?" said Mike. "Something tells me they may come after us eventually."

"We could," said Burke. "But this snow is not going to make for easy driving. And we seem to be doing pretty well on skis."

"It's only twenty miles to the arena," said Gardner. "And we need a workout."

"I bet it'd be faster on skis," said Trance. "What do you say, Coach?"

"I say let's do it—but no showing off. Some of us can't quite hold the pace we used to. One of us, anyway."

Burke and Steve had been carrying the others' skis and poles in their rifle slings. In less than a minute they were back in the road, skiing in a long line with Trance at the front and

Vern at the back. They gave a thumbs-up to their friend at the first gate as they sped through.

About a hundred yards later, they could see a pair of men in work gloves and chaps and hard hats waiting by the side of the road. As they went by, one of them waved, and fired up a chainsaw to cut the final notch—a big red pine toppled gracefully across the road behind them.

"What the hell was that?" asked Gardner, who was in the back of the line nearest Vern.

"Oh," he said. "A little insurance, just in case anyone's following."

For the next five miles, shortly after each intersection, they passed another pair of men, each team in full safety gear, and another tree toppled behind them. When they reached the main road to Burlington, Vern saw Sylvia standing by the side of the road, dressed in her cherry-red snowmobile leathers and shouting into a cell phone. She gave him a little wave and a thumbs-up. But he wasn't the only one who'd seen her. Trance, at the head of the line, slid to a hockey stop, and skied over to Sylvia, looked at her for a second, and then wrapped her up in a big hug.

"I'll catch you guys," she yelled to the rest of them. "You know I can."

28

"I was a little worried that after we pulled those tricks with their scoreboard last time, they might tighten up the cyber-security?" Perry was saying. "But no worries. I think we'll be able to improve the evening's proceedings at, um, our leisure? In fact, it should be easier since we're inside the big dome this time, not outside?"

He was sitting with Vern, Trance, Burke, and Gardner in an empty computer lab at the university journalism school, which was actually about four blocks from the Gov. Leslie R. Bruce Facility. The skiers looked serene—a red glow on their faces.

"Here, you can see the live feed from the hall," Perry said, pointing to another monitor.

"Where's the crowd?" asked Vern. "The place is empty."

"The snowstorm might have something to do with that?" said Perry. "They managed to get about six hundred people, in a school bus convoy that followed a snowplow. So they're seating them all around the podium, and the cameraman will keep it a tight shot all night so it looks like the place is filled."

"Can you show the whole thing so everyone watching at home will see how pathetic it is?"

"Yep—there's a remote-control roof-mounted camera that I can switch to. But I'll probably only get to use it once before they turn it off, so I'll wait for my cue."

"Okay," said Vern. "Burke, Gardner, time to get into the suits. You're Trance's federal escort for the evening. Here's your badge—you'll have to share, and it's not even real FBI. Contractors. *Sub*contractors. Get going. Trance, you're going to have to wing it, but I think the pictures on Dave's hard drive should help."

"Hello, Vermonters," the governor was shouting, as people on all sides waved American flags.

"Hello, Vermonters. As you can see, we've got a tremendous crowd here at the Gov. Leslie R. Bruce Facility tonight for our big Celebration of America. I'm amazed so many of you made it out through our snowstorm—ha, they talk about global warming! But I know that for every person here, a hundred of you are gathered by your TV sets and iPads. This is truly a night for Vermonters to celebrate our two-hundred-twenty-seven-year-long connection to the greatest country in the history of the world, the United States of America. So let us begin by rising—you at home can join in too!—for the playing of our national anthem."

All eyes turned to the JumboTron, where an animated American flag was waving—until Perry hit a key back in the journalism building and it was replaced by the image of Jimi Hendrix in blue beads and red headband, onstage at Woodstock. The crowd in the hall stood for the whole three minutes and forty-nine seconds of wild feedback; when it was over, the governor, looking a little flushed, said, "The great thing about America is that it is a melting pot where people of all kinds can perform their rhythmic music.

"Now, ladies and gentlemen, a very special treat. Joining us tonight via closed circuit broadcast is . . . none other than . . . the Secretary of State of the United States of America, the Honorable Rex Tillerson."

The jowly visage of the onetime Exxon CEO filled the JumboTron—he was smiling and waving at the crowd, who were smiling and waving back.

"Good evening, Governor Bruce, and good evening, people of Vermont!" he said, beaming. "I want to say that I've never had the chance to visit Vermont due to the fact that you have no deposits of oil or natural gas, but I do know that you have a number of very fine filling stations."

"Thank you, Mr. Secretary, for joining us here tonight. And thank you for all the help you've given us in recent days in tracking down the terrorists in our state!"

"We're always eager to help fight the war on terror—and I hear that we managed to rescue that pretty young Olympian from the terrorists who'd been holding her."

"Yes, Mr. Secretary—and Trance Harper will be with us in just a few moments."

"Well, give her a big hug for me. Now, I think we've got a special treat for you tonight. I hear that any second, fifteen of our Air Force jets will be flying overhead in formation, just to give you Vermonters a reminder of what freedom sounds like. Military parades are an important part of our country again— we paid for it, after all, and we're not afraid to show our might!"

"Um, Mr. Secretary, sir, I fear we had to scrub that mission because we're having a big snowstorm here, and the planes are grounded. But maybe we could give *you* a sense of how much noise we can make up here. Folks, can you join me? U-S-A, U-S-A, U-S-A."

On TV, thanks to a strategically placed microphone, the chant sounded loud, as if tens of thousands of people were joining in, instead of the six hundred clustered around the governor at the far end of an empty hall.

"I know all real Americans thank you for that witness," the secretary of state said. "And I just want to take this chance to tell anyone out there who might be thinking of voting for secession just what a bad idea it is. Your federal government supplies you with your Social Security check, your disability, your Medicare—think about that. I know that some of my ancestors tried to secede from the Union a long time ago, and I know that they wish they hadn't because it didn't work out so well. The great thing about America is, everyone has a chance to change it. Every person, every corporation, everyone is on an equal footing in this great land. As that great Vermonter Daniel Webster said, 'Liberty and Union, Now and Forever, One and Inseparable.'"

"Thank you, Mr. Secretary!" said Governor Bruce. "And I just want to say, you're invited up here to the Green Mountain State any time you want to come."

"God Bless the United States of America," said the secretary of state.

As his picture disappeared from the JumboTron, a new image appeared on the screen: a live shot of Trance, still in her green spandex, standing next to a man in a dark suit wearing sunglasses and appearing to speak into his lapel.

"Burke's hamming it up a little, I'm afraid," said Vern. "I mean, sunglasses?"

"Still, the governor looks relieved," said Perry, and indeed, on the monitor they could see him embracing Trance.

"Ladies and gentlemen, most of you saw our hometown hero Trance Harper on TV last night, explaining the web of terror that has fostered this so-called independence movement," he said. "I'm sure she's still worn out from her ordeal, so we don't actually need her to say anything, just to wave at you so you can see she's okay."

"Actually, Governor, I'm feeling fine," said Trance, as she cut toward the mike with Burke and Gardner running interference. "And I'm getting better at this public speaking thing—I think this is about my fourth speech this winter, which would also be about my fourth speech ever. So hopefully it will be pretty good.

"Better than last night, anyway—because last night I was feeling a little pressure. Here, let me show you. Most of you saw this picture on your TV"—up popped the video of Trance, speaking woodenly: ". . . *terrorists made me say things I did not believe.*"—"What you didn't see was this other video of the same scene, which my friend Perry should be able to show you now."

Instantly there appeared a wide shot, with Trance still reading—but this time Dave was standing at the edge of the frame, his Glock pointed at her head. A gasp went up from the crowd in the hall, and just at that moment Perry hit another button—silently the roof of the great hall began to slide open. It didn't take long for the governor to notice, partly because snow began to swirl in through the opening, caught in the floodlights around the upper deck. On TV, though, viewers simply saw the image of Trance at gunpoint, and heard her speaking live.

"As you can imagine," said Trance, "what I said last night was not true. It was dictated to me by Agent Dave and Agent Chet, who are not quite FBI but definitely government, and who were holding me in the upstairs barracks at the Ethan Allen Firing Range. Thanks to my friends Vern and Perry, to my former teammates on the Vermont biathlon squad, and to a bunch of other people for setting me free earlier today. None of them are terrorists, or anything like terrorists. The only people who have pointed a gun at me, or handcuffed me, or burned down houses, or done anything at all like that, are federal and state officials. They're not terrorists either—I think they're mostly just in over their heads."

By this point, the great dome of the Bruce Facility was half open, and the snow was streaming in. Perry flicked another button, and suddenly a camera mounted in the rafters for overhead views turned on, showing the great empty arena with the small cluster of people huddled at the far end. A low whining noise was audible in the background, like an oversized mosquito, and then suddenly over the lip of the stadium came a motorized hang glider, circling around the empty seats. It towed a banner: "The gods of the valleys," and seconds later another of the craft appeared, this one with the other half of the message: "Are not the gods of the hills." As they began to descend to the artificial turf, a third ultralight soared over the edge of the roof, trailing a banner that read: "Drink Heady Topper." It buzzed the crowd around the podium, and the pilot dropped hundreds of coupons for free pints of the state's most famous ale, which sent people scrambling into the aisles.

"What you hear is the sound of freedom," said Trance. "I've heard those great jets the secretary of state was talking about, and they may have their place, but here in Vermont the sound of freedom is low, quiet, small. It doesn't drown out everything else."

Two state policemen finally managed to push past Burke

and grab Trance, and the governor pushed his way back to the microphone.

"Fellow Vermonters," he began—but suddenly his mike went dead, and the JumboTron showed instead a picture of Vern and Perry back in the classroom full of computers.

"Hello, Vermonters. I imagine the state police may want to find us too," said Vern. "We were going to wait till after Town Meeting Day, but I think we've made our point, and we might as well go off to jail. Don't worry too much about us— the same legal team that represents Ms. Sylvia Granger of Starksboro has agreed to take on our cases as well. So—Chief Augustus—we're in room 332 of the journalism building, and we're ready to answer for our role in helping flood the Walmart.

"Until the police arrive, maybe we can tie up a few loose ends for you TV viewers. First of all, Daniel Webster is not from Vermont. He's from New Hampshire, which is a different thing altogether. Beyond that, I said the other night that I had absolutely no interest in running an independent Vermont. But I would like to point out that I have received an interesting e-mail from the fourth-grade class at the school in Weybridge proposing that the national tree of Vermont be the maple, the national animal the catamount, and the national drink a glass of milk. If and when I'm able to resume broadcasting, via the Internet from a new studio I've heard about in Starksboro, I will be promoting all three of those suggestions, though I think we should perhaps break the

beverage category into juvenile and adult. I will be campaign-
ing for craft-brewed beer as the state drink for those of us
above the age of twenty-one—and frankly, I have noticed
that in other countries they seem to get away with a lower
drinking age. But those are discussions for the future, if we
even decide we want to think about our own small nation.
Listen to your neighbors at town meeting, and follow your
hearts.

"And Perry, I think you have some things to add too?"

"Only one, really," he said. "Our website has actually been
up more often than not the past few days, and I've been tally-
ing your choices for a new national anthem. I admit that I
was a little worried about how many people were voting
for 'Moonlight in Vermont' from the 1943 film by the same
name. It's a fine song, but a little . . . So I'm happy to announce that the number one choice for Vermont's national
anthem, and actually by quite a wide margin of 14,321 votes,
is . . . 'O-o-h Child,' first recorded by the Five Stairsteps in
1970. It peaked at number eight on the Billboard Hot 100,
and it's been covered by dozens of artists since, including the
version by Dino in 1993 that made it to number twenty-seven
on the charts. We're going to hear the version by Miss Nina
Simone, sometimes called the High Priestess of Soul, who
was born Eunice . . ." At that moment the camera showed a
policeman grabbing Perry by the arm and yanking him away,
but not before he pushed one more button on his laptop, and
suddenly the camera was showing the arena once more, the

floor now white with snow, and the growling contralto of the Carolina-born singer filling the hall.

> *Someday we'll get it together and we'll get it undone . . .*
> *Someday when the world is much brighter . . .*
> *Someday we'll walk in the rays of a beautiful sun.*

People danced, people threw snowballs, people tried to get Trance's autograph as the police led her away. The governor stood by himself at the podium, pulling the lever that should have caused the dome to close.

29

"I call to order the two hundred thirty-eighth annual town meeting of the town of Starksboro," the town clerk and moderator said. "We have two major items on the warrant this year: a motion to buy a new road grader, and a motion to advise the legislature on seceding from the United States. But first, as is our custom, announcements. Lunch today will be provided by the sixth graders at the Robinson School, who are raising money for their trip to Quebec City. It's beef stew, and I'm told all the ingredients are local. Are there other announcements? Mr. Larson?"

"The plow hit my mailbox during the storm last week and I think the town should replace it."

"Thank you, Mr. Larson, that should probably be raised during new business at the end of the meeting, but I would also recommend you talk to the highway superintendent during lunch. Anything else? Chief Granger."

Sylvia, who was sitting next to Trance in the last long row of metal folding chairs, rose. "I'll make the fire department report later—and I'm warning we may need an appropriation for new radios. But first I just want to give my thanks to everyone who came out to fight the fire at my house, and who helped me later. As you know, the state's insurance company is going to build me a new place to live. But, thanks to my lawyers, they're also worried about any mental distress I might have suffered. I explained to them last week that my mental distress would best be treated by nice warm water, and so they kindly offered to build a community swimming pool next to the school. I signed a paper saying that that would take care of my troubles, so construction will begin early this summer and probably be finished by winter. See you all there."

She sat down and squeezed Trance's hand as people applauded.

"Thank you, Chief Granger. If there are no further announcements, then let us begin discussion on the first question we face: Should the people of Starksboro advise the state legislature to consider seceding from the United States of America . . ."

AUTHOR'S NOTE

An advantage to writing a fable is that you get to append a
moral to the end. In this case it's not "We should all secede."
Instead, it's that when confronted by small men doing big and
stupid things, we need to resist with all the creativity and wit
we can muster, and if we can do so without losing the civility
that makes life enjoyable, then so much the better. So far,
Americans have distinguished themselves in the age of
Trump: the first full day of his presidency saw millions of
(mostly) women in pink pussy hats on the street, followed in
subsequent days by sights of conscientious Americans flock-
ing to airports to protect immigrants, or thousands of New
York bodega owners shuttering their shops for a day in protest
of the new regime's Muslim ban. This nationwide unity of
dissent is just what the situation demands.

Secession, by contrast, has a limited but interesting recent history. Vermont actually had a minor-league attempt at
a secession movement about a decade ago, but it collapsed

when the organizers colluded with a collection of rancid southern racists. California's CalExit movement may be, circa 2017, the current most popular version, driven by the fact that the fifth-largest economy on earth has the same two senators as Wyoming or, well, Vermont. Anyway, we're early into the Trump dispensation—if things turn truly sour, you're all welcome to come to the Green Mountain State. We'll teach you to drive dirt roads in mud season and make sure you get a welcoming case of hoppy ale on your doorstep; almost any of you, in turn, would make this place a bit more diverse. . . .

The characters in this book aren't based on actual people (though I did borrow the names of a few of my favorite local journalists for the press conference scenes). For example, although Vermont's governor, Phil Scott, is a Republican, he's been a stalwart opponent of Mr. Trump, for which many thanks.

I'm grateful to many friends for their help. My colleagues at 350.org and throughout the climate justice movement have taught me most of what I know about activism (though those who want to cause trouble effectively can shorten their learning curve by picking up the new organizing manual, *This Is an Uprising* by Mark and Paul Engler). My colleagues at Middlebury College, led by the remarkable Laurie Patton, sharpen my thinking—and Mike Hussey and the college's crack crew of ski-trail groomers let me dream of skiing like Trance, or at least Vern. Radio may seem an old-fashioned medium to some, but not to me—in fact, my daughter Sophie has recently taken her first job in podcasting, at WGBH, one reason I'm currently so fascinated by the sound of the human voice appearing out of the ether. As always, my main sounding board, and my main joy, is my wife, Sue Halpern (an actual novelist).

Many thanks to early readers of this book: Sam Verhovek, Andrew Gardner, Naomi Klein, May Boeve, Jamie Henn, Peter Sarsgaard. Gloria Loomis and Julia Masnik agented with their usual panache. And it is a particular pleasure to be re-united with David Rosenthal, who edited my very first book, *The End of Nature*, all the way back in the 1980s. He figured out how to make this story stand up; I'm very grateful.

ABOUT THE AUTHOR

Bill McKibben is the author of many books on the environment and related issues—his first book, *The End of Nature*, is generally regarded as the first book about global warming for a general audience. It has been published in twenty-four languages and was serialized in *The New Yorker*, where McKibben was once a staff writer. His work appears regularly in newspapers and magazines around the world.

As a founder of 350.org, the global climate campaign, McKibben has helped organize demonstrations in 191 countries, and was a leader of the fight against the Keystone pipeline and for divestment from fossil fuels. His work has been recognized with, among other prizes, the Right Livelihood Award, sometimes called the "alternative Nobel." He has had a new species named in his honor, *Megophthalmidia mckibbeni*, which some biologists describe as a "pesky woodland gnat."

McKibben has lived in Vermont for many years, roaming the mountains and forests on both sides of Lake Champlain in all seasons. The Schumann Distinguished Scholar in Environmental Studies at Middlebury College, he was named Vermonter of the Year in 2012. He lives with his wife, the writer Sue Halpern, and their dog, Birke, on the edge of the Green Mountain National Forest's Breadloaf Wilderness.